Ordinary Mishaps
and
Inevitable Catastrophes

ALSO BY BOOKI VIVAT

FRAZZLED

Everyday Disasters and Impending Doom

BOOKI VIVAT

FRAZZLED

ORDINARY MiSHaPS and inevitable CATASTROPHES

HARPER

An Imprint of HarperCollinsPublishers

Frazzled #2: Ordinary Mishaps and Inevitable Catastrophes
Copyright © 2017 by Vissra Vivatnamongkon
All rights reserved. Printed in the United States of America.

Library of Congress Control Number: 2017934812
ISBN 978-0-06-239881-9

17 18 19 20 21   CG/LSCH   10 9 8 7 6 5 4 3 2 1
❖
First Edition

For anyone still trying to figure out the new, unexpected, and unknown

Ordinary Mishaps
and
Inevitable Catastrophes

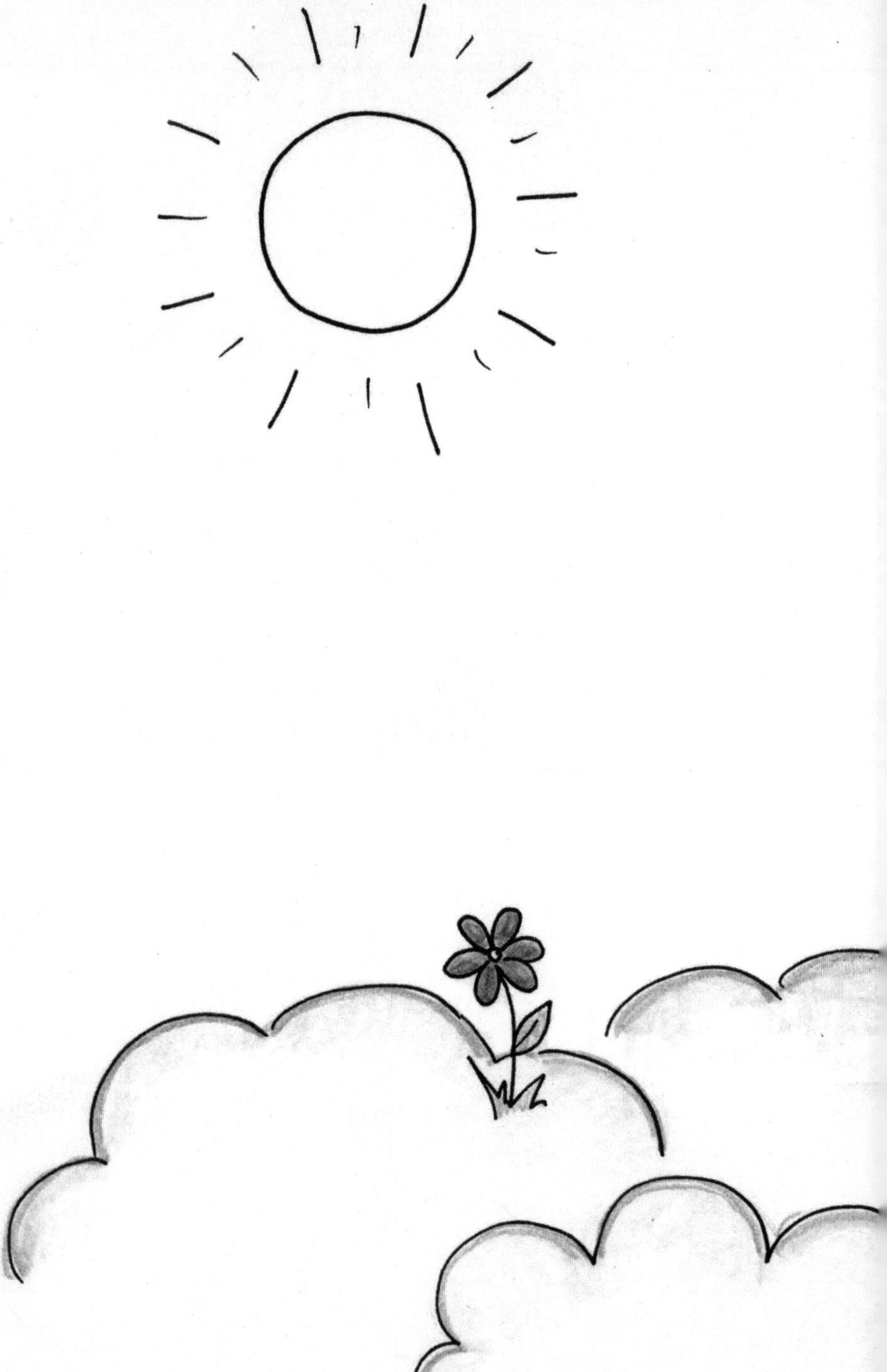

The best feeling in the whole wide world is when things go EXACTLY the way you want them to.

It feels like everyone is
rooting for you,

like you can do anything you set your mind to,

like the Universe is
on your side
and nothing can
POSSIBLY
go wrong.

Until, of course,

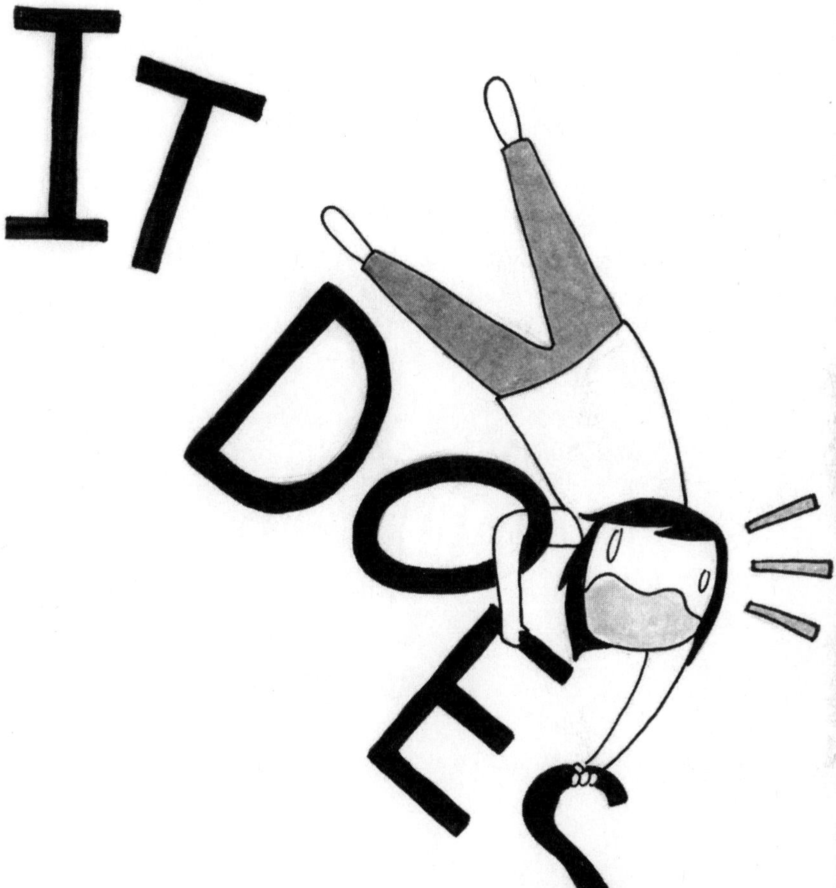
IT DOES.

That is usually how things work out for me. Being in middle school doesn't help.

I can say that now that I'm in it. It's confusing. It's chaotic. It's the center of madness! We're all just trying to survive, but teachers still expect us to learn stuff while we're here. Talk about unreasonable expectations! Well, if I've learned anything so far from being at Pointdexter Middle School, it's THIS. . . .

If something CAN go wrong, it definitely WILL!

This isn't just a fact—it's LAW.
(Go ahead. Look it up.)

Some guy named Murphy said it once and everyone knew he was right, so they made it "official."

I hereby declare this *Murphy's Law!*

It also happens to be TRUE. I know this from years of personal experience.

For example, FIRST GRADE.
I think I hit my peak in first grade.

Every week, our teacher, Mrs. Han, would
make us run laps around the playground,
and I would always finish first. I was
the fastest kid in the whole class!
Faster than all the boys.
Faster than all the girls.
Faster than EVERYBODY.

Then Mrs. Han left to
go teach English at the
high school. Suddenly,
everything changed.

Our new teacher made us run around the park next to the school instead. The PARK—with its sketchy fields . . .

EW! DOG POOP!

and annoying potholes . . .

and terrible steep hills.

I never finished first EVER AGAIN.

It goes to show that just when you think things are going your way . . .

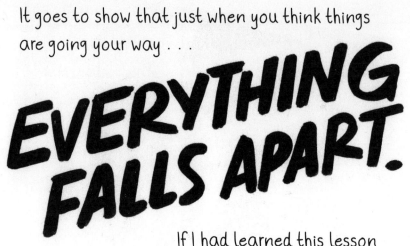

EVERYTHING FALLS APART.

If I had learned this lesson when I was younger, maybe it all could have been different.

Instead, I got too caught up in the fact that, for a little while, life in middle school was starting to LOOK UP.

Things at home weren't so bad.

Peter and I weren't fighting as much as we used to—except when it came to who got control of the TV remote.

Let's face it. That was the type of family conflict that could NEVER be resolved.

Clara was being nicer to me lately too. Her birthday was coming up and I was pretty sure she thought good behavior would help her get a better present out of Mom. Maybe it would work. . . .

Mom was always in a better mood whenever the three of us got along.

9

School was SCHOOL, but at least the cafeteria food started tasting a little bit better.

They said it was some kind of new statewide lunch initiative, but Maxine, Logan, and I liked to think it had something to do with our short-lived lunch revolution.

Maybe it made a difference after all. It definitely changed things with Ms. Skelter.

She became a lot nicer and even let us share snacks in study hall as long as we kept the classroom clean.

Even though this was middle school and
things weren't easy, I was somehow surviving!
I was even considering running for class
president—ME!

Things were going so well that, for a second there, I forgot about all the stuff that could (and would) go wrong. All I could think was that THIS was my time.

ABBIE WU was up-and-coming, on the rise, THE ONE TO WATCH!

Then, REALITY HIT.

First of all, I found out that Cody Donaldson was planning to run for class president.

CODY DONALDSON

good dancer
über-popular
TOTAL JERK

Cody was the worst kind of popular kid—mostly mean and very self-involved.

Most of us didn't like him very much, but he had somehow secured a place for himself at the highest level of middle school society. Needless to say, he was the kind of kid who could do pretty much anything he wanted.

I didn't stand a chance. Plus, even if I DID—
the more I looked into being class president,
the less I WANTED to be class president.
Apparently it wasn't just about making posters
and getting votes!

Leading the student
council meetings
every week . . .

cooperating with the
adults at school . . .

talking onstage
during assemblies?

That didn't sound like me at all!

To be honest, it didn't sound much like Cody either. Even though I didn't want to be president myself, I definitely knew that I didn't want HIM to be.

He couldn't even spell "president" right on his campaign posters. Apparently knowing how to spell check was not a qualification for representing the student body.

Then again, nothing made sense in middle school.

On top of all that, we found out that Cody was planning to crash the presidential debate with an

The possibility of being forced to dance in front of the WHOLE SCHOOL was reason enough for me NOT to run.

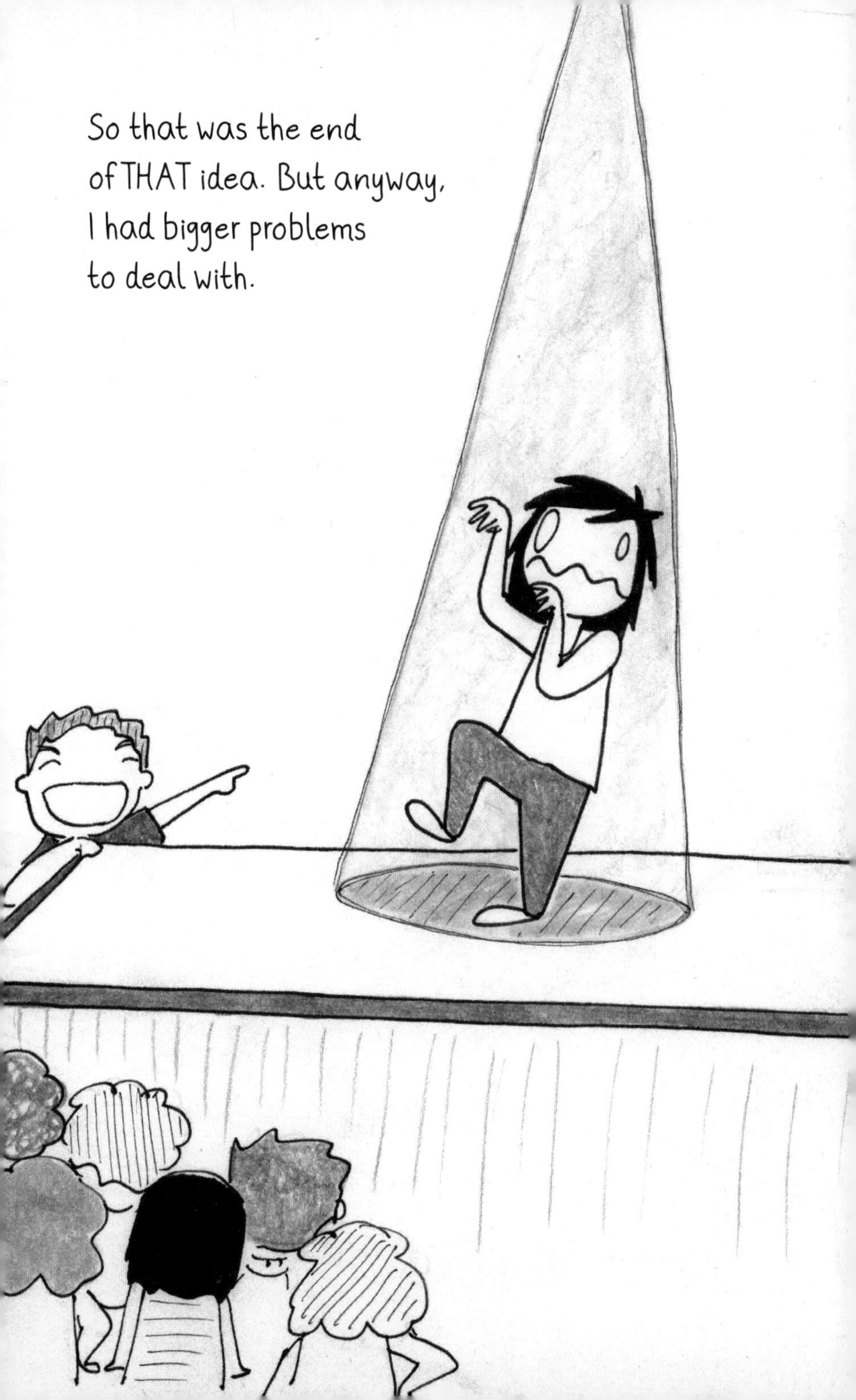
So that was the end of THAT idea. But anyway, I had bigger problems to deal with.

CHAPTER TWO

There had to be some kind of secret power that came with being the youngest child.

SUPER CLARA

IRRESISTIBLY CUTE!
UTTERLY INFALLIBLE!

Before Clara, I had had a few years of being the youngest, but as soon as I became the middle child, I had NO power at all.

If I asked for something . . .

Mom just said she'd "think about it." When Clara wanted something, 98.7% of the time SHE GOT IT.

Her birthday this year
was no exception.

KITTY!

For Clara, this meant
a furry new best friend.

For me, it meant
TROUBLE.

It's important to note that I have never been a fan of cats. They scratch too much, and they're always lurking around like they're about to carry out some evil scheme.

The Spencer family next door has TWO of them. They are fat and they smell. Much like their owners, they have been torturing me for years.

GET HER!

HA HA HA

UGH, CATS.

I hate them and they hate me.
And now I have to LIVE with one!

For some reason,
Clara wanted to name it

MR.FELIX
McSNUGGLES
the
THIRD.

I don't know why he needed such a silly last
name or why he would be called "the Third"
when he was technically our FIRST cat. It was
the most obnoxious pet name I'd ever heard,
but he technically belonged to Clara,
so she got her way—as usual.

I never even wanted a cat in the
first place, but despite all my protests
and warnings, we had become a

 **CAT FAMILY.**

That changed EVERYTHING.

Mr. Felix McSnuggles
the Third, like his name,
was a LOT to handle
and made life at home
MUCH more complicated.

Mom even added extra cat care responsibilities
to the . . .

 **Wu Family CHORE WHEEL!**

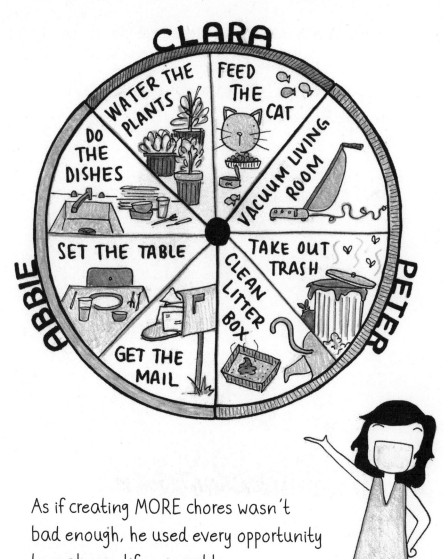

As if creating MORE chores wasn't bad enough, he used every opportunity to make my life miserable.

Feeding Felix was the worst job on the chore wheel. It wasn't a particularly hard task on its own, but Felix's interference made it unexpectedly difficult.

ow!

To top it all off, once he finished eating, he always begged for more food and threw a fit when he realized he wasn't getting any.

For some reason, the rest of the family didn't seem to have any trouble with it—or with Felix, for that matter!

It was just ME.

In fact, Felix was welcomed into the family almost immediately. Even Peter, who was generally more of a dog person, said he didn't mind having a cat.

Maybe that was because the cat didn't seem to mind HIM . . .

whereas Felix made it very clear that WE were enemies.

all MY stuff —
RUINED!

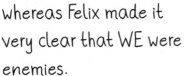

ARGH!

While I was dealing with major cat problems at home, my troubles at school were just beginning.

It all started with

LOCKERS.

Lockers were a rite of passage—or at least, they should have been. Everyone in middle school was supposed to get a locker (the ONLY perk of now having MORE textbooks), but of course, our school didn't have enough.

According to Peter, there was a running joke about the long-awaited (and perpetually delayed) completion of Pointdexter Middle School's sixth-grade locker pavilion.

But then, at our last school assembly, Vice Principal Kline told us that they had FINALLY finished construction and would assign lockers to ALL sixth-grade students within the week!

Our whole section of the auditorium started cheering.

SETTLE DOWN!

Vice Principal Kline could barely finish her announcements.

She could hardly blame us.
This was REVOLUTIONARY.

No more broken zippers!
No more back pain!
No more sore arms!

We were finally getting LOCKERS—

WOO-HOO!

THAT was something worth celebrating!

Little did I know that for me, the celebration would not last long.

CHAPTER THREE

They passed out our locker assignments in homeroom. Most people raced to find their lockers at the end of the period, but not me.

I had a PLAN. I had been waiting years for this. To me, it was more than just a place to put my books and lunch box and extra pencils. It was something I could make MY OWN, and I wanted everything to be PERFECT.

I went home and practiced on an old lock
I found in the garage until I could open it in
my sleep.

Turn 3x to the right.
STOP ON 28.

Turn one full turn
to the left, passing
the 1st number.
STOP ON 12.

Turn to
the right.
STOP ON 8.

Pull down
and...
voilà,
UNLOCKED!

Mom dropped me off at school early the next day so I could get settled. When I found my locker, it was in the ideal spot—

just far enough from the boys' locker room to avoid that sweaty-air smell,

just close enough to the cafeteria to give me a head start on getting in line at lunch.

Everything was going according to plan.

I had the combination memorized, and thanks to all that practice, the locker opened without a hitch!

But, of course, Murphy was right.

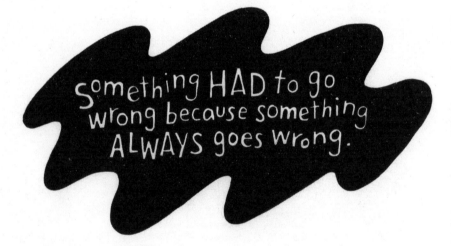

Something HAD to go wrong because something ALWAYS goes wrong.

When I opened that metal door, it was worse than any of the worst-case scenarios I could've imagined.

Worse than fumbling
over the lock.

Worse than the door
being a little dented.

Worse than having
a locker near Ryan
Savage—the meanest,
rudest, nastiest bully in
all of sixth grade.

It was ALREADY TAKEN!

Not only had my beautiful, perfect, private new locker been hijacked—it had been hijacked by a

MONSTER.

NOTEBOOKS COVERED IN PERMANENT MARKER DOODLES

LOOSE PAPERS SPILLING OUT OF THEIR BINDERS

HALF-EATEN CANDY (BUT NOT EVEN THE GOOD KIND)

SMELLY LUNCH BAG WITH VERY SUSPICIOUS STAIN

TEXTBOOKS WITH BENT SPINES AND DOG-EARED FOLDED PAGES

EMPTY WATER BOTTLES THAT NEED TO BE RECYCLED

PENS AND PENCILS SCATTERED EVERYWHERE

39

There was even this crumpled-up paper bag stuffed in the back that looked sketchy and smelled funky. I had no idea what was inside. It could've been anything!

I tried to make Logan investigate, but he refused to touch it, so testing was limited and results were inconclusive.

Whatever it was, it definitely didn't belong there . . . in MY locker!

Who was this LOCKER THIEF? Why take MY locker?

We needed a . . .

STAKE🔍UT!

We set up base at a planter near the new lockers.

Maxine brought disguises from the drama club's prop room, but in the end, we decided they might be a little too suspicious.

So we just played it cool . . .

and waited . . .
and waited . . .
and waited.

Just when it seemed hopeless, someone appeared!

THE LOCKER THIEF

The locker thief wasn't at all like I'd imagined.

EXPECTATION

REALITY

If I didn't know any better, I would've thought she was just a regular student. . . .

Except NONE OF US recognized her!

Even Lana Alvarez had no clue who she was—

and Lana was the type of person who knew
EVERYONE.

Her anonymity only made her more suspicious.
Whoever she was, I had to figure out how to get
her out of my locker.

The gang and I spent most of the lunch period trying to think of a proper plan of action to take back my locker. Most of our ideas were a little too complicated. . . .

But eventually, we came up with

THE PLAN.

I still had my practice lock from home in my backpack. All we had to do was wait until the coast was clear, take out all her stuff, and replace the lock.

Okay, so it sounded harsh—

But it's not like we were planning on throwing
her stuff away! I just wanted my locker to
be MY LOCKER, and that meant finding
somewhere else for HER stuff.

Maybe a bag with a polite
notice of relocation
or something like
that. . . .

The end-of-lunch bell rang. All the yard duties
were on high alert, wrangling students who
were moving too slowly and screeching at
everyone to get to class!

Our plan would
have to wait.

With this locker problem totally unresolved and fresh in my mind, the last thing I wanted to do was think about

SCIENCE!

It wasn't so much that I hated science—I just didn't GET IT. The only thing that made it semi-interesting was . . .

MR. WALTERS.

He wore thick glasses that made his eyes look buggy and his hair was always sticking up like he had just put his finger in an electrical socket. The look was very "mad scientist." Some people thought it was too cliché, but it kind of worked for him.

He started the class with his usual pep.

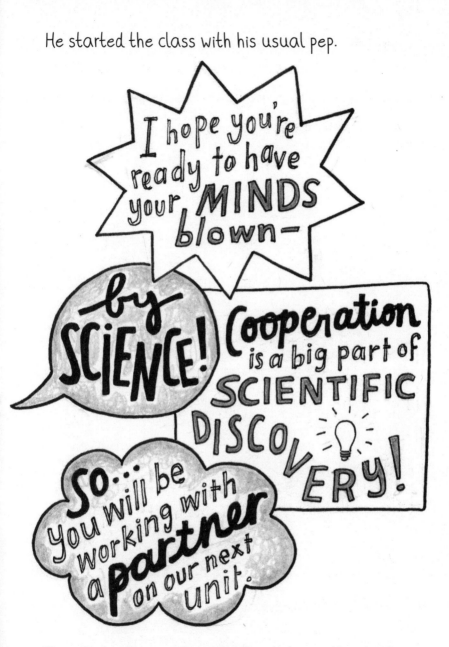

The whole class groaned. We all knew the deal.

Teachers never let you choose your partner, and unless you were very very lucky, you usually got someone you never really wanted to get at all.

I did NOT have a particularly good track record when it came to partners.

When Mr. Walters started reading
off the list of pairs, I realized
that he was putting us together

ALPHABETICALLY!!!

Alphabetical order was the WORST.

In elementary school, I used to have to line up
behind Trevor Whipple.

GOTCHA!

PFFFT

He liked to fart on people FOR FUN.

Then, for a while, there was a girl in my class named Alice Wong.

Teachers ALWAYS mixed us up, even though we were NOTHING alike.

Oops! Haha! I can never tell you two apart!

I didn't know who I would be stuck with this time, but as Mr. Walters got closer and closer to the end of the alphabet, I began to brace myself.

LESLIE TYSON + ANDY TU, RON VALDEZ + AMY WINSLOW

ABBIE WU AND...
ABBIE WU AND...

ABBIE WU AND...
JESSICA WYATT!

Who was that?

The name didn't sound familiar at all. As if he was reading my mind, Mr. Walters motioned to the back of the room and said,

" I almost forgot. We have a **NEW** student! Welcome to **SCIENCE** class, where we learn about the world around us and try to have **FUN** while doing it — at least...

PERIODICALLY! "

While the rest of the class laughed (or at least pretended to laugh) at his corny joke, I turned to look at my new partner—and my whole stomach d r o p p e d.

It was HER! THE LOCKER THIEF.

CHAPTER FOUR

I couldn't pay attention to anything Mr. Walters said after that. How could I be expected to learn SCIENCE under these circumstances? This was NOT just another coincidence. This was the Universe playing a mean joke on me. This was Murphy's Law at its very worst. This was a catastrophe. This was inevitable. This was . . .

I had to do SOMETHING, so I waited until class was over to talk to Mr. Walters and beg him for a new partner.

I thought I did an okay job pleading my case.

It didn't do much good, though. He just wouldn't budge!

"THE SCIENCE GODS HAVE spoken!

JESSICA WYATT

ABBIE WU

You're PARTNERS now.

give it a chance!

This CLASS [and LIFE, for that matter] is all about experimenting with the UNKNOWN."

* YOU NEVER KNOW... you might LEARN something!

Mr. Walters was all about trying new things, but I didn't like them AT ALL. New things were messy and confusing and unpredictable. I was NOT a fan of new things.

Plus, this threw a huge wrench into

THE PLAN.

If I was really stuck with this new girl as my science partner, I couldn't exactly go through with our scheme without causing MAJOR problems.

I wanted her out of my locker, but I also wanted a good grade in Mr. Walters's class, and now Jessica Wyatt was a part of that too. I hadn't even met her yet, and she was already affecting the course of my life!

If I didn't work with her as my partner, I could fail science and get stuck in middle school for another year.

Nooooooooooooooo

That was my doomsday scenario. I could NOT let that happen. So I was STUCK.

I zoned out for a minute in front of the locker . . .

~~HER locker.~~

~~MY locker.~~

OUR LOCKER?

As I contemplated my unfortunate fate and racked my brain for any sort of loophole I may have overlooked,

SHE SHOWED UP.

There was a long, empty silence.

* Was she :

SCARED   SURPRISED   ANGRY   NONE OF THE ABOVE   ?

I had no clue. Then, she did the STRANGEST thing—she laughed a little, shook her head, and said,

Oh! Did they give us the **SAME LOCKER** ? Haha!

. . . like it was NO BIG DEAL!

She suggested we go to the office to sort things out—

the office

of all places!

I don't know what school she went to before, but this confirmed it: she was definitely new to Pointdexter. Every kid here knew that the office was never as helpful as you wanted (or needed) it to be.

shhhh!

They mostly just made copies of things and told you to be quiet while you waited.

Plus, the chairs in the office were really uncomfortable. They made them that way on purpose.

Still, she seemed sure that it would solve our problem, so I thought we'd give it a shot. After school, we met at the locker and walked to the office together.

I couldn't think of what to say and she seemed okay with neither of us saying anything.

It was AWKWARD.

When we told the lady at the front desk that we had a locker problem, she didn't take us seriously at all.

I wasn't surprised. Adults never seem to think our problems are all that important, so they aren't much help when it comes to solving them.

I was ready to give up, but Jess had another plan in mind.

She started explaining our situation to the office lady, Ms. Hayes, and somehow convinced her to help us! Everyone knew that the office was notoriously unhelpful, and yet . . .

Well, you see....

I had never seen anything like it. Was she some kind of adult-whisperer? Could she get them to fix it? For a split second, I thought this might work itself out—until Ms. Hayes looked up from her computer, lowered her glasses, and said,

SO... (I could tell by her pause that it was not good.)

It looks like there was a little MISTAKE with the locker assignments... WHOOPS! Unfortunately, all the lockers have already been assigned and there aren't any empty ones left. There's NOTHING we can do!

I think she said something about "sharing" too, but I didn't feel like listening after that.

The way I saw it, this was a sign. After all, the whole mix-up happened because there was some unexplainable glitch in the system when the lockers were assigned

ALPHABETICALLY!!!

I had suspected for years, but this solidified it.

The alphabet was out to get me.

CHAPTER FIVE

When I left school, all I could think about were my options—or rather, lack of options.

I started thinking and walking and thinking and walking. Before I knew it, I was in front of Antonia's Bake Shop! It was as if some kind of cosmic force had guided me there to try to make me feel better.

Or it could have just been my stomach.

Inside the bakery, Maxine and Logan were sitting at our usual table doing their homework.

I must have been in bad shape when I walked in because as soon as they saw me, they instantly launched into BFF Comfort Mode.

ABBIE!

Ah, what happened?

Tell us everything.

Istvan could sense it too. Before we left that day, he stopped by our table with a pastry to-go box in hand!

Here. You look like you could use it.

Turns out, Istvan wasn't just the world's best pastry chef. He was a mind reader too!

Inside was a perfectly baked chocolate tart— just for me.

It was exactly what I needed.

When I got home, I set the box down on
the counter and turned my back on it
for a second.

But I was not alone.
Nothing was safe anymore.

Mr. Felix McSnuggles the Third
was on the prowl, and a second
was all he needed. . . .

MWAHAH

This time, he had crossed the line.

I had no choice but to bring it up in our

Mom got the idea for family meetings from some weird parenting book her friend bought her. At first, we all thought it was a joke, but Mom ended up liking them so much that family meetings became a permanent thing.

WU FAMILY MEETING, NOW IN SESSION!

If they were ever going to take my complaints about Felix seriously, it would be in a family meeting.

The hardest part was figuring out how to bring it up. It didn't help that I could feel Felix staring at me from across the room . . . taunting me with his manipulative, beady eyes.

For some reason, this family meeting felt longer than all the others. It's like we were in the Twilight Zone, caught in a looped discussion about chores and allowance and extracurricular activities.

But then, I finally saw the chance to say something.

They had to know the truth! I had to tell them!

HE'S DOING IT ON PURPOSE TO PUNISH ME!!!

Felix clearly had it out for me, but the whole family just thought I was being paranoid.

... but he's so CUTE!

He's just a CAT...

Aunt Lisa was usually on my side, but this time, I wasn't so sure.

After all . . . she was a "cat person."

Mom tried to make me feel better. . . .

I know you don't really LIKE Felix, but he's part of the FAMILY now.

You have to try and make the BEST of it! Who knows? Maybe you'll end up getting along!

But I could tell that she didn't really GET it.

The problem was, no one was EVER around to see Felix terrorize me. He conveniently timed his attacks for when they weren't looking.

Felix was DIABOLICAL.

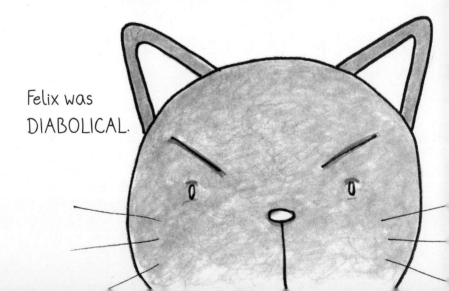

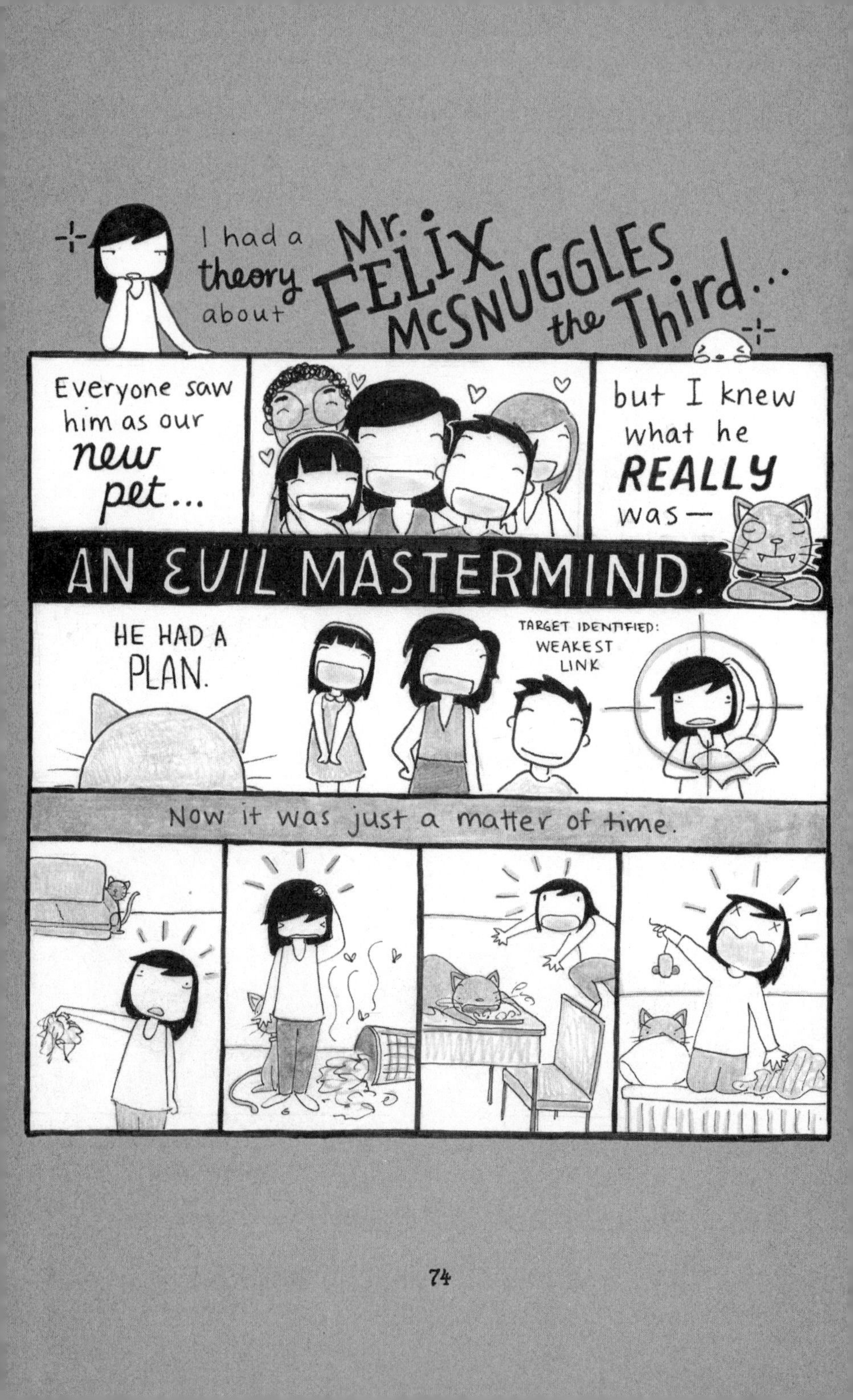
I had a theory about Mr. FELIX McSNUGGLES the Third...
Everyone saw him as our new pet...
but I knew what he REALLY was—
AN EVIL MASTERMIND.
HE HAD A PLAN.
TARGET IDENTIFIED: WEAKEST LINK
Now it was just a matter of time.

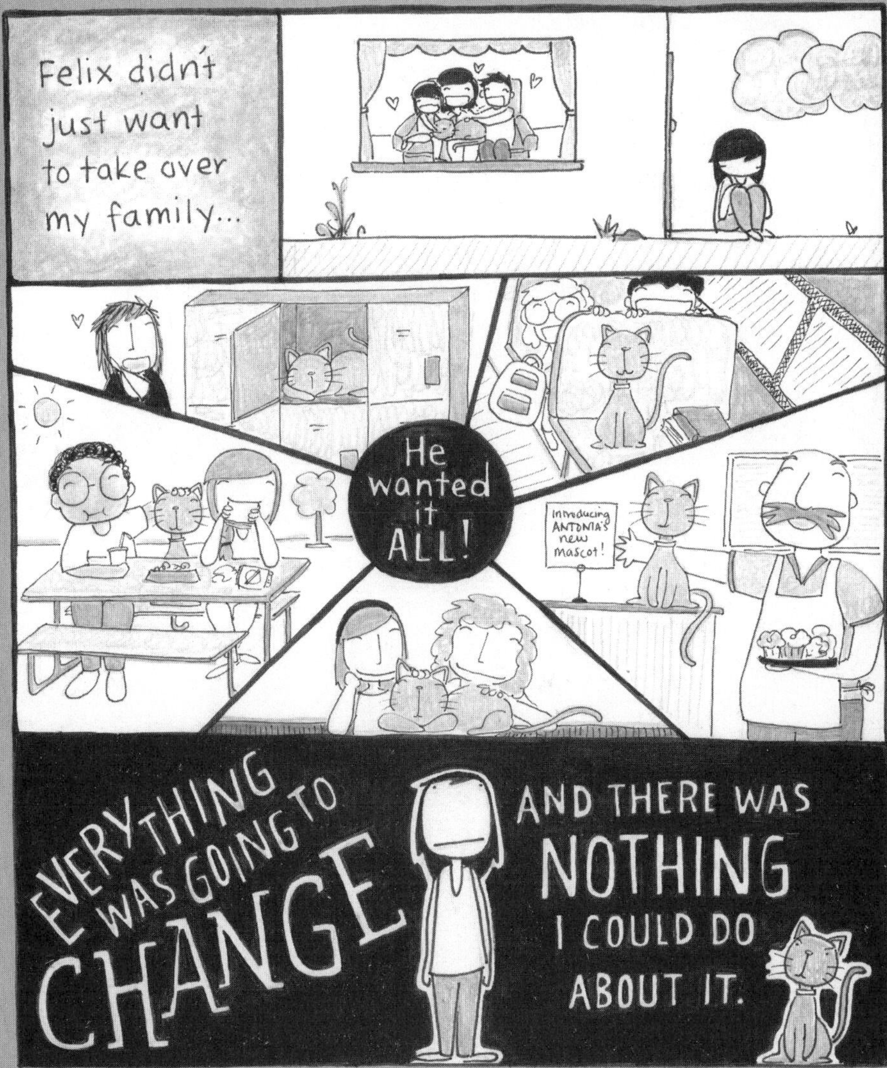
Felix didn't just want to take over my family...
He wanted it ALL!
Introducing ANTONIA'S new mascot!
EVERYTHING WAS GOING TO CHANGE
AND THERE WAS NOTHING I COULD DO ABOUT IT.

Aunt Lisa was a big fan of family meetings, and she had her own unique take on how to deal with Felix.

Just imagine that you and Felix are the SAME. you are the Cat. He is you. WE ARE ONE.

Though a bit unconventional, she was a VERY convincing person.

Somehow she got us to try this new meditation technique with her.

Still, it felt silly to imagine any of us being "one" with Felix.

After a while, Aunt Lisa let us open our eyes and said,

Don't you feel like the VIBE is better now?

And, if I was honest, I really DID feel a little better. Maybe Aunt Lisa's new technique actually worked. . . .

Or maybe it was the fact that after all that,
she brought out a surprise she'd been saving
for dessert—a huge confetti
cake baked from scratch for
us, and some
fancy cat treats
for Felix.

It wasn't exactly
the same as a
fancy chocolate tart from Antonia's, but
it was still really really REALLY good. Plus,
seeing Felix munching happily on his treats gave
me a brilliant idea.

At night, Felix liked to sneak into my closet and spy on me through a curtain of dresses and coats.

Then, just as I was on the verge of sleep, he would bolt out of his hiding spot and pounce on my head!

But NOT this time.

This time, I slipped him a few extra treats before bedtime. My offering of savory fish-shaped snacks must have satisfied him enough to leave me alone for the rest of the night.

SUCCESS!

The whole cat snack experiment made me think that maybe Mom had a point—and, in her own way, maybe Aunt Lisa did too. I HAD to make things work.

unpredictable science partner who also happens to be my unwanted new locker buddy (and may even be kind of nice?)

conniving new mortal enemy who isn't even human

But it wasn't going to be easy.

CHAPTER SIX

I didn't LOVE the idea of sharing a locker, but I wasn't sure I could survive without one.

Why did we need this many textbooks in middle school anyway? They weren't just regular-size books either—they were GIGANTIC. Each one felt like a huge, boxy boulder that would crush me if I wasn't careful.

We didn't even use them most of the time. We just had to bring them to class to prove we were "prepared."

The bottom line was that there was ONE locker and TWO of us. Somehow we had to coexist.

Before school, I practiced giving my speech about sharing the locker and somehow making it work.

But when I ran into Jess at school, she was already a step ahead. She had cleared out half the locker for me—no books and papers crammed into each other, no empty candy wrappers, no mysterious smelly package!

Maybe I should've been happy about that, but instead, I just felt confused. Jess didn't seem bothered by the fact that sharing a locker meant less space, zero privacy, and forced cohabitation with a total stranger. In fact, she seemed totally fine with the whole thing!

How was she so okay with it? Then again, in the short amount of time I had known her, she also seemed like the kind of person who was okay with pretty much anything.

I just didn't **GET** HER.

So I decided to execute my own secret scientific study to try to figure her out. In class, Mr. Walters had been talking a lot about the scientific method—this fancy, official way of figuring out the truth.

If I wanted real answers about Jessica Wyatt, maybe science really WAS the way to get them!

STEP #1 : QUESTION

Who is Jessica Wyatt REALLY?

How is she so CHILL?

Mr. Walters said that science was all about trying to "know the unknown," and at this point, Jessica Wyatt was DEFINITELY an unknown.

STEP #2: HYPOTHESIZE

Maybe THAT was my real problem with Jessica Wyatt. No one knew who she was or what she was like. In many ways, NOT KNOWING was the worst part.

I HAD to find out.

STEP #3 : EXPERIMENT

Between sharing a locker and working as partners in science class, I had plenty of chances to test out my theories, make some observations, and gather data.

STEP #4 : OBSERVE + RECORD

The thing is, it all led back to the same baffling conclusion—

STEP #5 : ANALYZE

Jess was not fazed by ANYTHING.

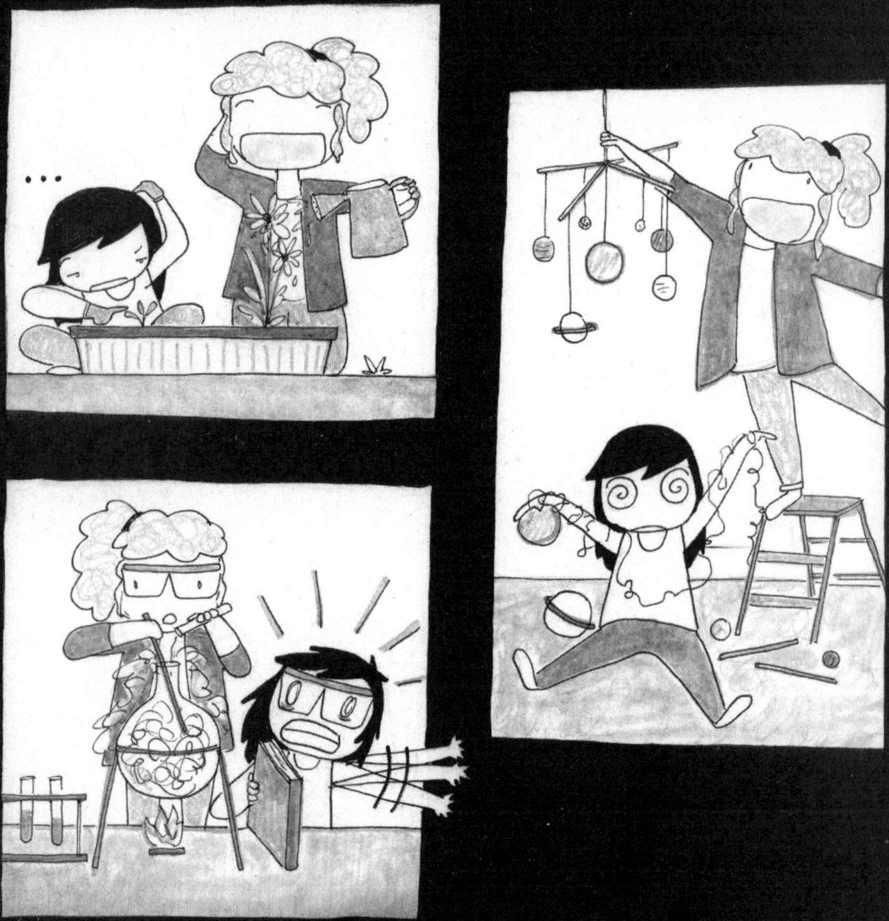
...

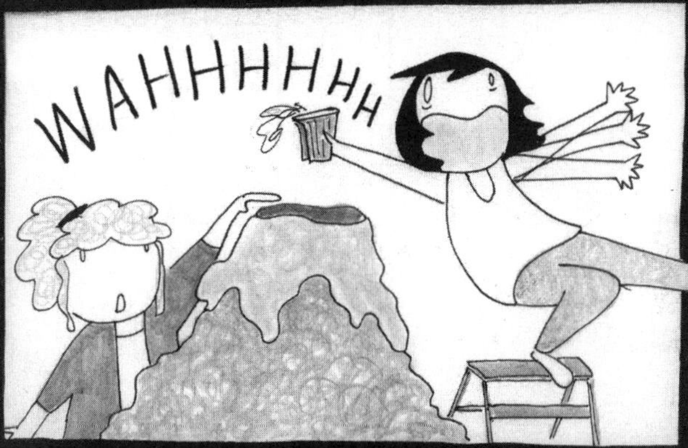
WAHHHHHH

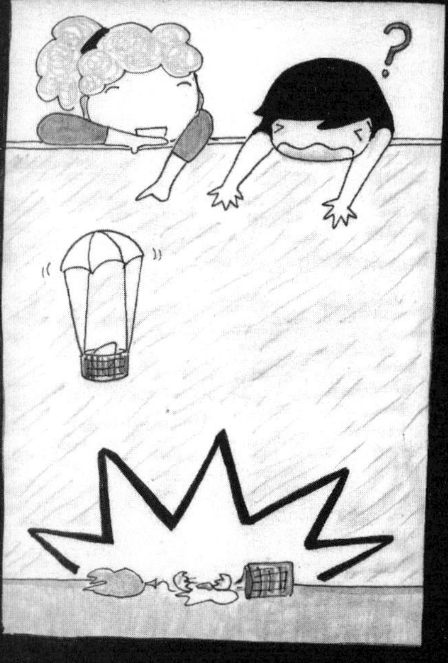
?

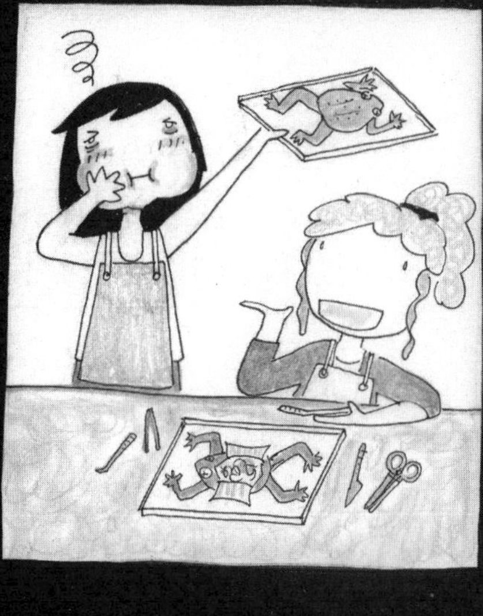

We'd been spending a lot of time together in class, but I hadn't managed to figure her out yet! From my research, I concluded the following points:

She was pretty nice . . .

not mean and snobby like the Spencer sisters . . .

or sadistic and cruel like that bullying jerk Ryan Savage.

She was sort of private and mysterious . . .

but never in that creepy way Danny Andrews was when he stared at you from across the room for too long.

She was very clever . . .

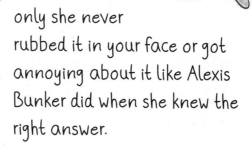

only she never rubbed it in your face or got annoying about it like Alexis Bunker did when she knew the right answer.

Jess Wyatt wasn't like most kids at Pointdexter. She was hard to read, and even after all my scientific observations, I still didn't know what to expect from her! Maybe I never would. . . .

STEP #6: SHARE RESULTS

The last step of the scientific process was to report my findings, but the whole experiment was not nearly as informative as I had hoped it would be. When I told Maxine and Logan about it, they seemed more curious than confused.

So curious, in fact, that Maxine went ahead and invited Jess to join us for lunch!

Maxine was very impulsive, so it didn't really surprise me when she asked.

Jess, on the other hand, was VERY surprised. She didn't hang around with anyone in particular and she didn't exactly fit into one specific group at school. She didn't really seem to WANT to either.

From all the data I'd collected about Jess Wyatt, I came to the conclusion that she would probably say no. She seemed to prefer being on her own and doing her own thing anyway.

But then she said . . .

um...

OKAY!

So I guess I really DIDN'T have Jess figured out.

At first it was weird having someone new at our table. For years, it had always been just the three of us.

We knew each other better than anyone else. Maxine and Logan probably knew me better than my own family, and I knew pretty much EVERYTHING about them.

I knew that Logan hated polka dots.

(They reminded him of a particularly traumatic case of chicken pox.)

I knew that Maxine carried around a piece of old chewing gum in a tiny plastic box for good luck.

(She swore it belonged to Julie Andrews.)

Sometimes I thought I knew them so well that I could tell what they were thinking, even if they didn't say it. But with Jess, I didn't know anything!

At first, I couldn't help but wonder if this would turn out to be the most awkward lunch EVER . . .

But it wasn't.

I thought it would be weird that we didn't
know anything about Jess and she didn't know
anything about us, but actually, NOT
KNOWING made things kind of interesting.

That day, we learned a lot about her—definitely more than I had through my secret scientific study.

likes pickles

listens to old records

knits (a lot)

obsessed with THE BEATLES

(especially George)

hates snakes

watches scary movies (for fun)

!!!

If someone had told me earlier that I would be sitting at a lunch table and sharing my chips with the kid who hijacked my locker, I would never have believed them. I guess that's what Mr. Walters meant when he said that life is unpredictable.

Considering how things started out between us . . .

LOCKER THIEF!!!

We actually got along okay.

Even sharing a locker wasn't nearly as bad as I thought it would be. I had to admit, it had its advantages.

One night I fell asleep doing homework.

Felix sensed my
guard was down.

He knocked my history book off the table and
hid it under the bed.

I didn't realize it was
missing until I was heading
to class the next day.

Mr. Monroe was a stickler when it came to being prepared, so I knew that I was going to be in

SO MUCH TROUBLE!

But then . . .

You can use mine!

problem solved!

That's how we came up with
the idea to share books.

We were already stuck sharing a locker. It
didn't make sense to have two copies of
the SAME BOOKS taking up space, so we
figured we might as well share those too!

I had to admit, it was
a pretty good idea.

On the other hand, life with Felix hadn't gotten better at all. It was almost WORSE.

Felix caught on to my snack strategy and was no longer responding to bribery.

In fact, he seemed almost OFFENDED by my attempts to control him and, out of revenge, launched a vicious campaign against me.

RAWR!!!

He ruined EVERYTHING.

It could have been a mortifying social catastrophe!

HAHAHA HA HA HA
HAHAHAHAHAHA HA HA
HAHAHA HA HA
HAHA HA
HA

Luckily, Jess came up with a temporary fix before anything bad could happen.

She saved the day!

It made me realize that, even if we were total opposites, Jess might not be such a bad person to have around.

CHAPTER SEVEN

One day, Mr. Walters seemed more excited than usual to start class. There was clearly something he wasn't telling us, and everyone was buzzing with rumors of what crazy idea he had in mind. He had a reputation for coming up with unconventional new ways of making science seem "cool and relevant."

When Peter had Mr. Walters as a teacher, his class went on a hike into the wild to collect and identify local vegetation for their biology unit.

Half the class ended up trekking through a field of poison ivy . . .

and the other half had a VERY close run-in with a wasps' nest.

Apparently Mr. Walters had considered it a "great learning experience," so it was hard to predict what he could possibly have planned for US.

Let's talk about...

INVENTIONS

Inventions are all about solving problems and making life better. We are surrounded by great inventions!

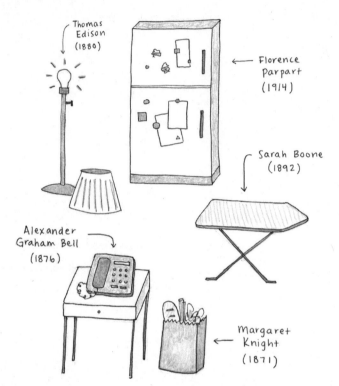

Thomas Edison (1880)

Florence Parpart (1914)

Sarah Boone (1892)

Alexander Graham Bell (1876)

Margaret Knight (1871)

But rather than just talking about these scientists and their revolutionary creations, I want you all to tap into your own creative energy and follow in their footsteps.

I'm proud to announce that Pointdexter Middle School will be hosting its very first

Invention Convention!

For your final partner project, you'll create your very own inventions and present them to all the sixth-grade science classes that day.

It's a big part of your final grade, so DO YOUR BEST!

Do your best?

DO YOUR BEST?!?!

What if my best wasn't good enough?
What if my best wasn't good at all?

The more Mr. Walters talked about it, the more
excited he got and the more convinced I was
that this project was going to be a complete
and total DISASTER.

Not only did we have to invent something
totally cool and new, we had to get onstage
and present it to everyone!

I thought that the class would erupt in protests and boycotts after Mr. Walters announced it, but actually they all seemed to feed off his excitement. I didn't get it!

THIS WAS MY WORST NIGHTMARE!!!

I didn't like big crowds or public speaking or stages, for that matter.

Plus, I wasn't an

I just used things
other people invented!

I didn't have any new ideas!
I didn't know how to make things work!

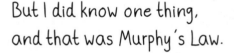

But I did know one thing,
and that was Murphy's Law.

There were so many things that could go
wrong. Why didn't anyone else see that? Even
Maxine and Logan bought into the hype of the
Invention Convention.

Maxine was more excited about the idea of being onstage in front of a built-in audience than the actual "invention" part of things . . .

BUT she was lucky enough to be paired with Alexis Bunker.

I bet Alexis had mapped out their whole project before Mr. Walters even finished the lesson.

Logan didn't seem bothered by the assignment at all. If I was a boy genius, I probably wouldn't be either.

Plus, he was partnered with Mira Shahin, who was insanely smart and a natural science whiz.

I later found out that, months ago, they had started running science experiments and building new inventions on their own—just for fun.

Imagine what they could do if they REALLY tried.

Unlike the others,
Jess and I had

Jess didn't seem too worried, but I knew we needed to get to work. That day, we headed to my house after school to get started on it.

On the walk home, I tried to warn her about what to expect.

Of course, when I told her, she was not fazed at all.

In fact, she thought all my stories about life at home were kind of funny!

I wasn't sure why.

Jess was an only child
and she had to move
around a lot because
of her dad, but even
then, her family
sounded pretty normal
compared to mine.

Most people who didn't know my family tended
to assume that we were calm and peaceful,
but in reality, we were anything BUT—

especially now that
Felix was part of the
family.

The second we stepped through the doorway,
Felix shot out from behind the sofa and
pounced on me as if I were some kind of
household intruder.

And THAT was only the beginning. Mr. Felix
McSnuggles the Third was in a particularly
vindictive mood that day.

We couldn't get anything done!

That was his plan all along. Maybe this was his way of punishing me for bringing a new person into the house without his approval. Or maybe he just had it in for me.

Whatever the reason, he was making it difficult to even THINK about our invention.

After a while, Jess said:

HE REALLY HAS IT OUT FOR YOU!

She actually agreed with me! For once, someone was on MY side.

Finally SOMEONE UNDERSTOOD!

When Jess started talking about her grandma's cat, Mitzy, it occurred to me that we might have more things in common than I originally thought

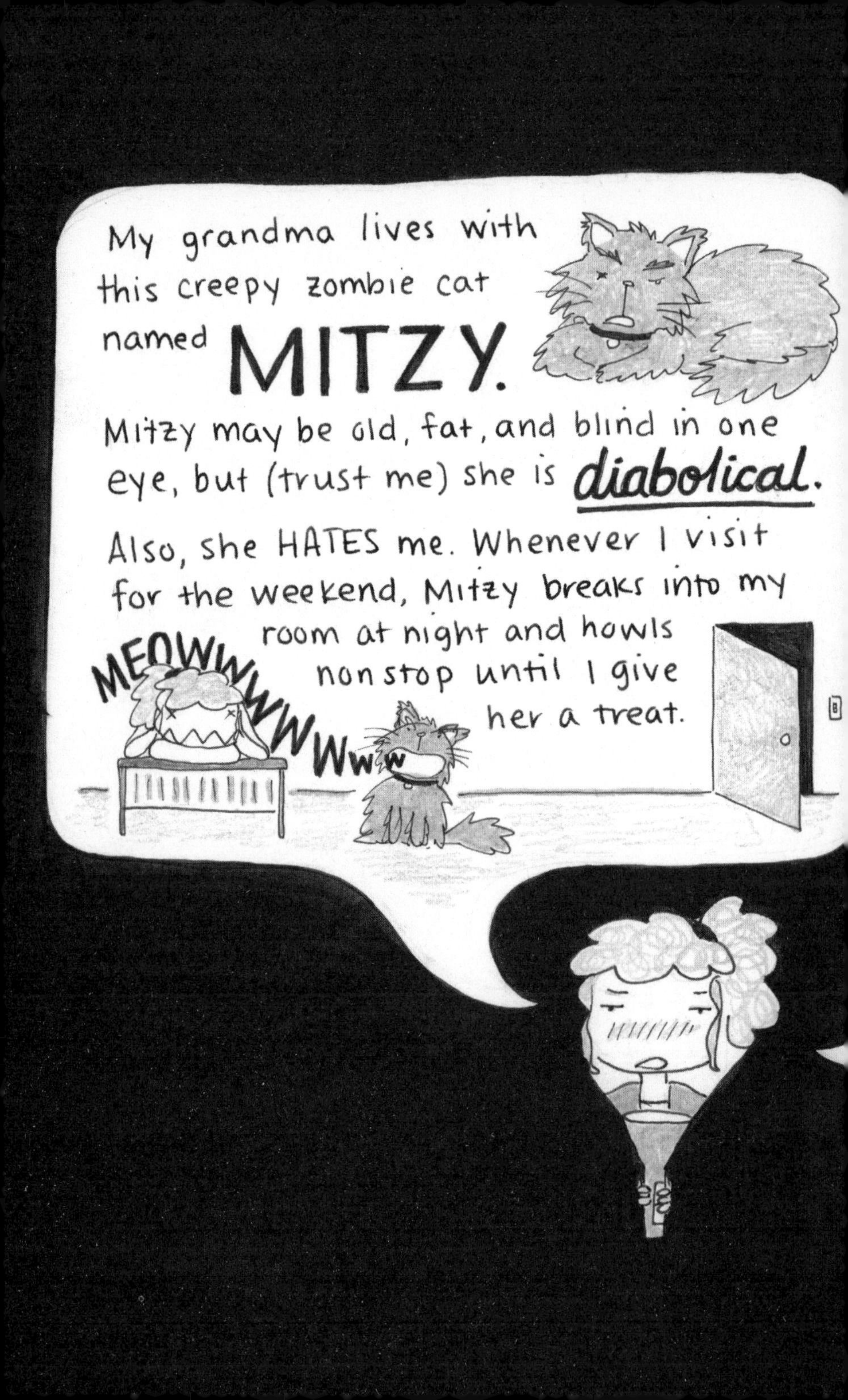
My grandma lives with this creepy zombie cat named MITZY.
Mitzy may be old, fat, and blind in one eye, but (trust me) she is diabolical.
Also, she HATES me. Whenever I visit for the weekend, Mitzy breaks into my room at night and howls nonstop until I give her a treat.
MEOWWWWWWWWWww

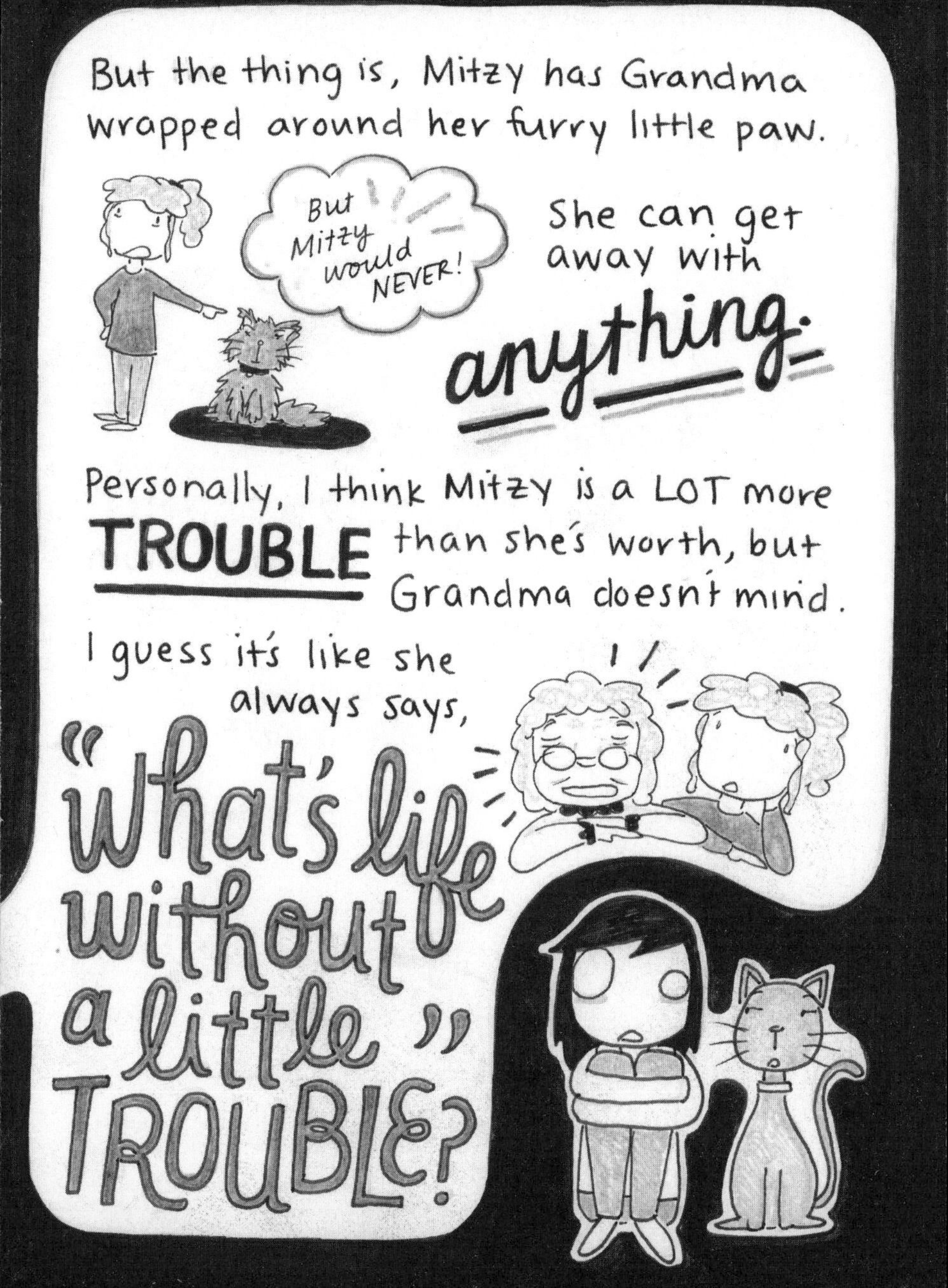
But the thing is, Mitzy has Grandma wrapped around her furry little paw.
But Mitzy would NEVER!
She can get away with anything.
Personally, I think Mitzy is a LOT more TROUBLE than she's worth, but Grandma doesn't mind.
I guess it's like she always says,
"What's life without a little TROUBLE?"

After that, things felt a little different between us. I guess this was what it felt like to find "common ground" or whatever.

She was the only one who seemed to really GET IT.

Maybe I needed to reexamine my original hypothesis about Jessica Wyatt. At first, I thought she was just a locker thief, my mandatory science partner, the new kid at school. I thought we would NEVER get along.

But the more we worked together and the more I thought about it, the more I realized that we were starting to become friends—or at the very least, "almost friends."

Too bad being "almost friends" didn't help
much when it came to our science project.

When Peter came
home from soccer
practice, we were in
the middle of what
seemed like our two
hundred fifty-seventh
bad invention idea.

#257

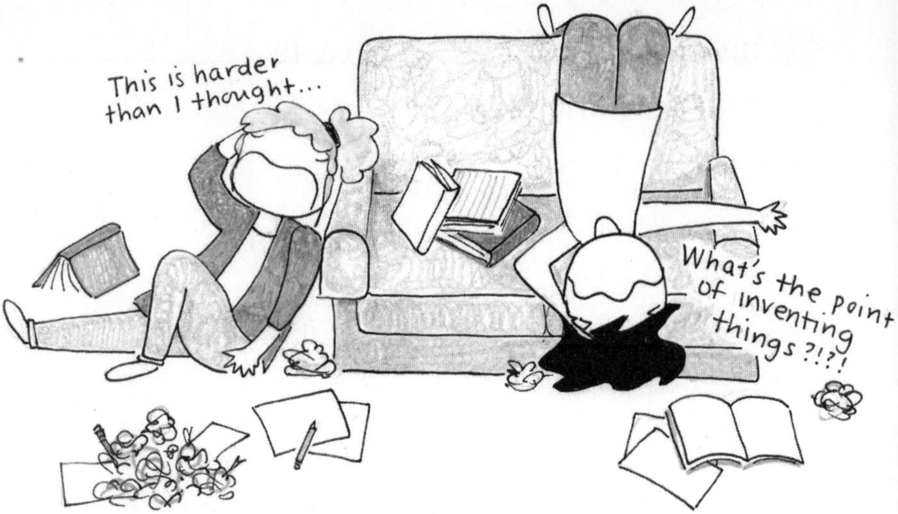
This is harder than I thought...
What's the point of inventing things?!?!

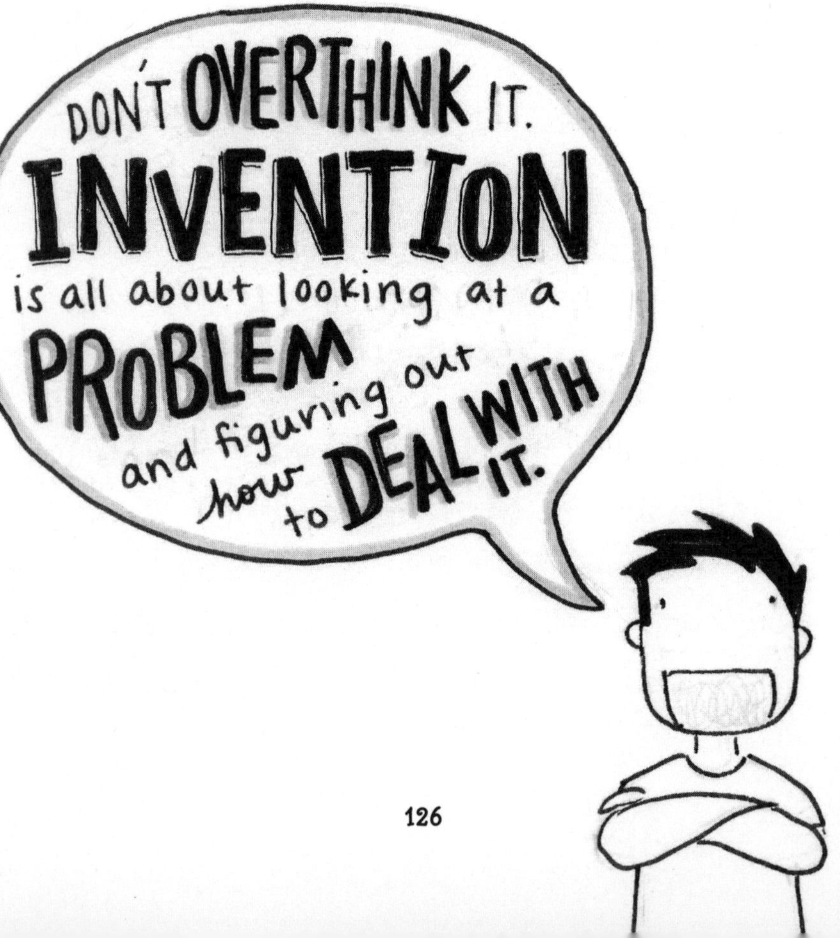
DON'T OVERTHINK IT.
INVENTION
is all about looking at a
PROBLEM
and figuring out
how to DEAL WITH IT.

He said it like it was such an easy thing, and it probably WAS for him. Peter could invent something in his sleep and still get first place at the Invention Convention.

I didn't ASK for his advice, but I guess what he said actually DID make sense. Peter always liked to stick his nose in my business.

Sometimes I couldn't tell if he was genuinely trying to be helpful or if he just enjoyed being nosy.

Later, he popped his head in the room and started nagging me about my chores!

Don't forget to feed Felix before Mom gets home. It's your turn!

Maybe being a big brother meant you were somehow both helpful AND nosy.

The truth is, I actually HAD forgotten, so it was probably good he reminded me. Mom always said I had a "selective memory" because it seemed like I conveniently forgot things I didn't WANT to remember.

And, well, I definitely didn't WANT to feed the cat. Even with Jess's help, feeding Felix was a NIGHTMARE.

There MUST be a BETTER way to do this!!!

As soon as those words came out of my mouth, something CLICKED.

I looked over at Jess and knew that, in that moment, we were thinking the EXACT SAME THING.

"There WILL be

...once WE think of one!"

That was the beginning
of the FEED-IT 5000—
the ultimate cat feeder.

Who would've thought?

I guess you never really
know when a good thing
is going to hit.

CHAPTER EIGHT

Finally, we had our idea—create the greatest cat food contraption in the history of Pointdexter Middle School . . . an invention so great it would make Mr. Walters cry when we finally revealed it.

GENIUS!!!

(He often got emotional over great scientific achievements.)

I was perfectly fine settling for a moderately successful presentation and a decent final grade, but Jess seemed to think this could be something much more than that—something GREAT.

Of course, I was always a little skeptical when things started going well, but Jess was so excited about our idea that my cynicism felt out of place next to her certainty.

She was so SURE of herself that her sureness trickled into everything else—including our science project.

It wasn't just her confidence that impressed me. It was her ability to keep that confidence even when things weren't always so great.

Once we started working, we quickly learned that building an invention was a lot more complicated than just coming up with the idea for one. . . .

But that didn't discourage her. Even when our ideas didn't work or things went wrong, she never doubted the fact that we would figure it out.

We worked on the project together almost every day after school.

It was strange how we could
look at the same exact thing
and see it completely differently.

AHA!

YES!

Somehow, though, that
was what made it WORK.

As the Invention Convention drew closer, we both knew there was SOMETHING missing. We spent hours trying to figure out what exactly that something was, but nothing fit. Then, right when we were ready to give up—

EUREKA!

It was so average and unassuming. We hadn't noticed it before, but there it was. . . .

Right there in
front of us.

Once we figured out that missing piece,
everything fell into place. It was complete!

Each part had a purpose, each step made
sense. It all fit together. Looking at it, I could
barely believe that WE were the ones who
made it, something totally new and totally
OURS.

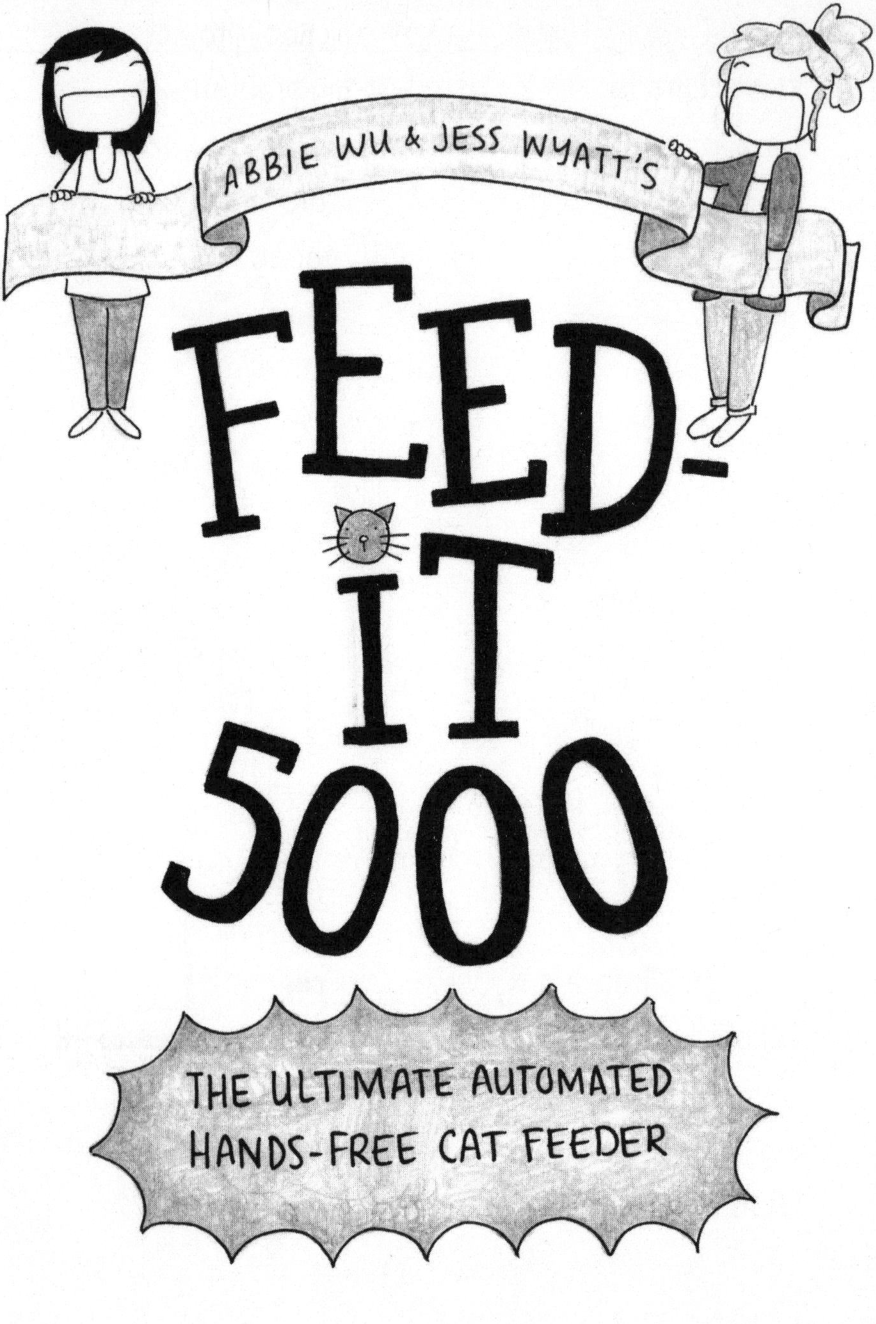
ABBIE WU & JESS WYATT'S
FEED-IT 5000
THE ULTIMATE AUTOMATED HANDS-FREE CAT FEEDER

It might have started out as a school project and a convenient solution to my problems feeding Felix, but when I looked at it now, in its completed form, it felt like more than just that. It was something kind of great.

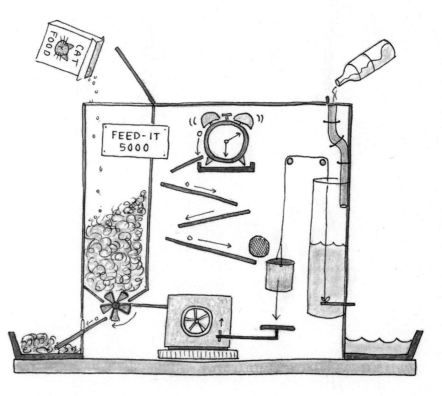

The real question was whether or not it WORKED.

Once it was basically complete, Jess wanted
to test it out as soon as possible, but I kept
looking for reasons to delay it.

A few more tweaks.

Some minor
adjustments.

Another round of inspections.

I double- and triple-checked each part
of the machine.

A weird, uncomfortable knot formed in my
chest as I looked over each step. The slightest
mistake or tiniest mishap could come along
and ruin EVERYTHING!

We worked NONSTOP to put it together. The idea of our invention not working was almost too tragic to consider!

If Jess felt the same, she didn't show it. It was almost like she knew something I didn't.

It's going to WORK OUT.

Where did she get that kind of certainty, and how could I get some?

When it was finally time to put the FEED-IT 5000 to the test, we crossed our fingers and held our breath.

144

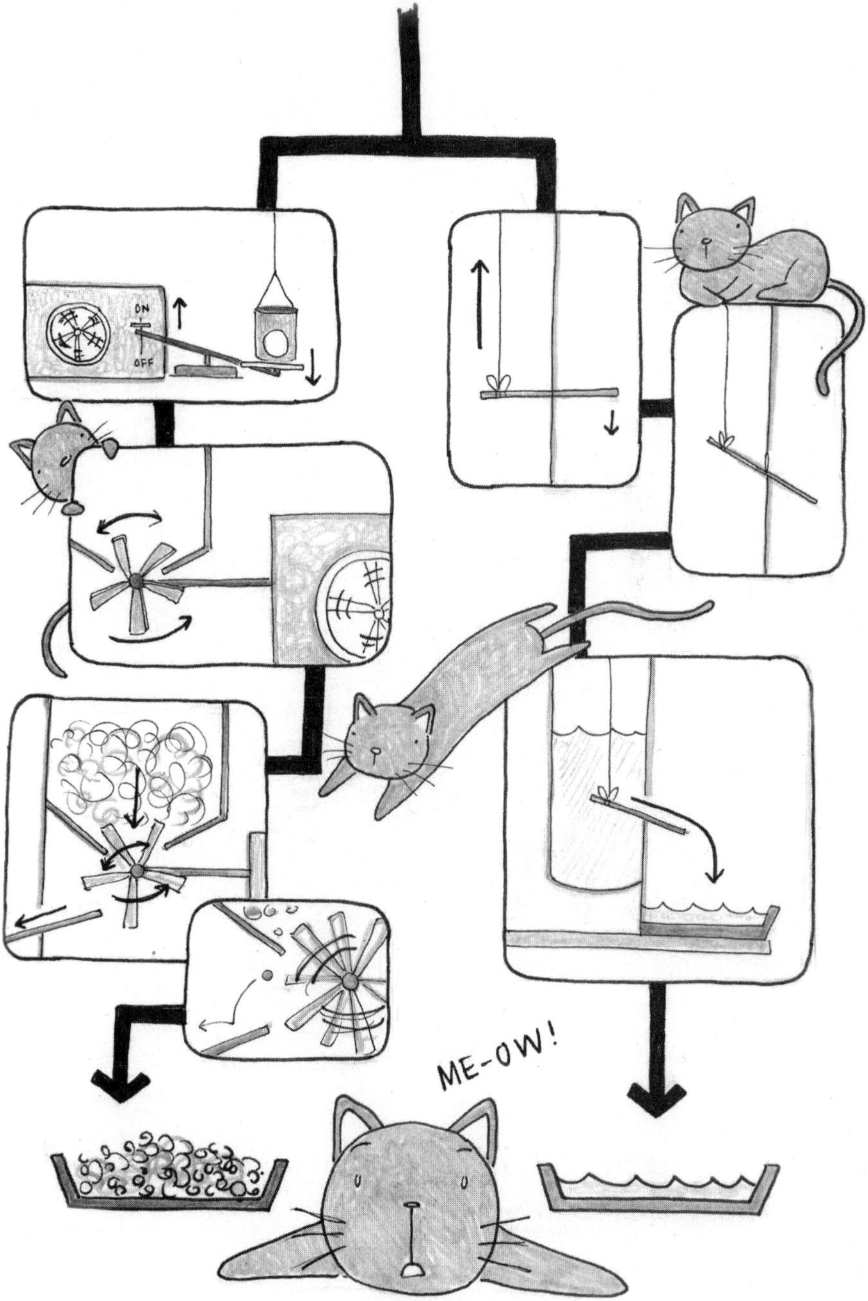
ON
OFF
ME-OW!

WE DID IT!

IT WORKED.

Felix, who had just caught on to the fact that he was somehow involved in the process, was surprisingly encouraging.

me-ow!

We tested it at least a dozen times after that—adjusting things here and there, adding a few improvements, making it better and better.

Instead of just nerves, I started to feel a rush whenever the machine worked. Each successful trial run felt like a small but significant victory.

I THINK WE CAN WIN.

Sometimes people say things like that just to say them— not because they're serious. But when Jess said it, she MEANT IT.

As we both looked over at our finished project, I secretly wondered if maybe she was right.

CHAPTER NINE

Leading up to the Invention Convention, it seemed like that was all anyone could talk about!

What's WITH them?

What are they so excited about?

Even the seventh and eighth graders started to notice that something was going on.

As much as I had dreaded it in the past, I couldn't help but get swept up in the excitement of it all.

It was hard not to!

GREATEST *inventors* OF ALL TIME!

There was still a part of me that worried about having to present our invention in front of everyone, but another part of me was actually kind of excited about it. Maybe Jess was rubbing off on me after all.

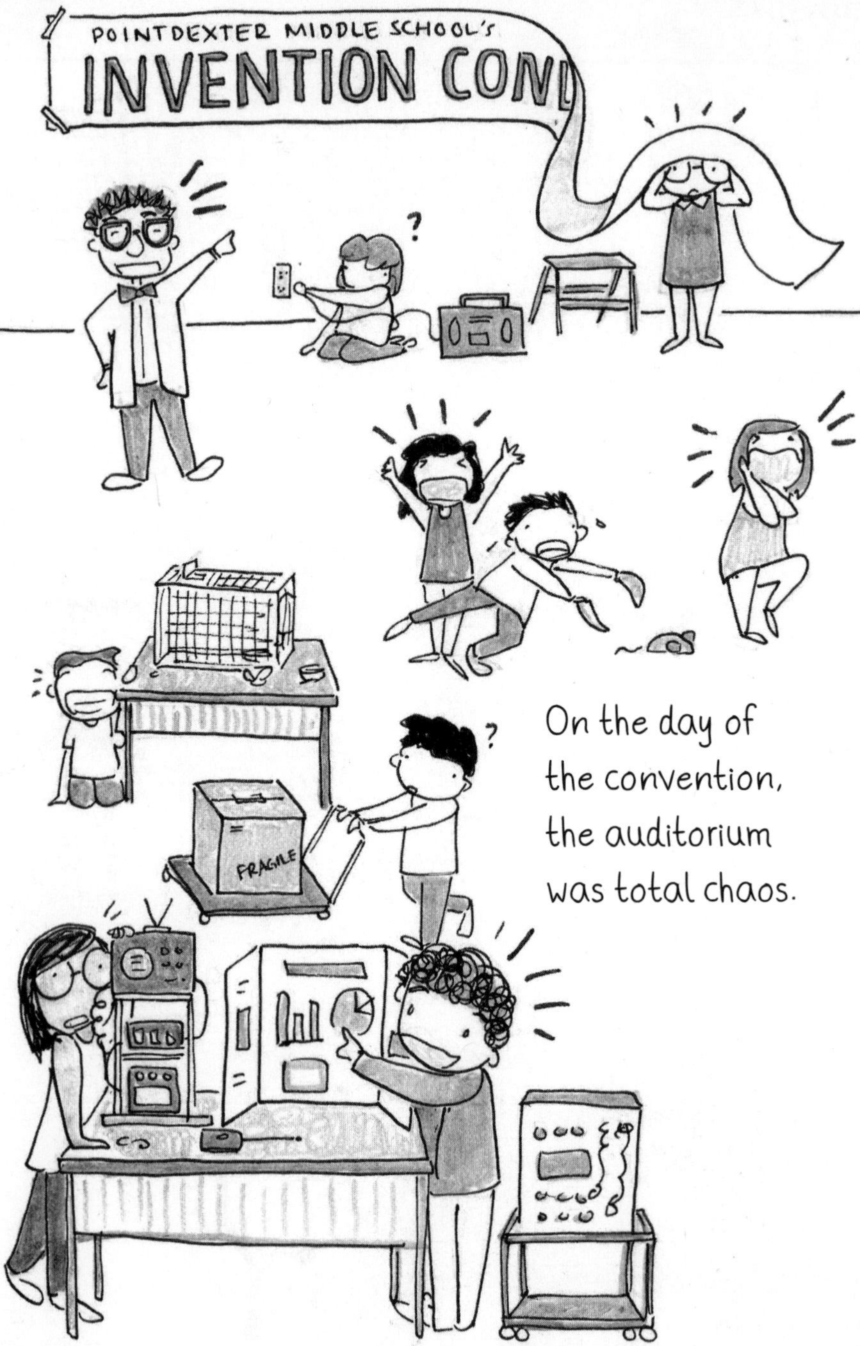
POINTDEXTER MIDDLE SCHOOL'S
INVENTION CON
FRAGILE

On the day of the convention, the auditorium was total chaos.

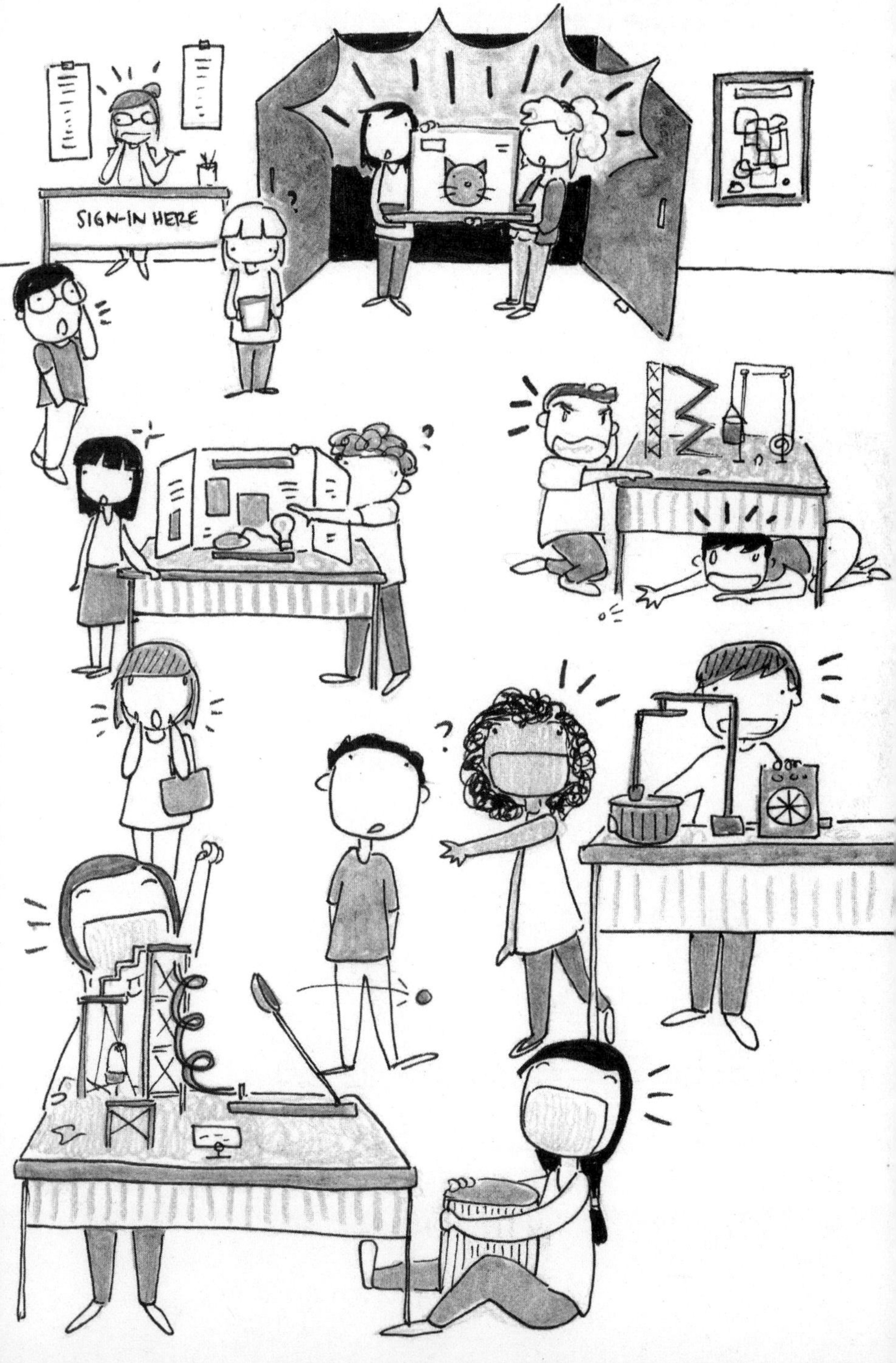
SIGN-IN HERE

Before we knew it, it was our turn.
We carried our project onstage and
started to set up
the presentation.

I couldn't tell if my heart was beating faster
because I was nervous or because the FEED-IT
5000 was heavy and hard to get up the stairs.
The stage was much higher than it looked, and
when I stared down at the crowd, I could see
everything and everyone.

They were all staring back.

YIKES!

I could feel myself start to panic.
Maybe Jess could too because
she gave me a nudge and a confident nod.

WE CAN DO THIS!

Before all this—before
the whole locker mix-up,
before we became science
partners, before even really
knowing each other—I probably wouldn't have
believed her. But now I sort of DID.

Once we started our presentation, the whole room was buzzing.

They loved it! It was a hit!

Everything was going according to plan. All that was left was to put the FEED-IT 5000 into action.

As soon as we finished setting up, there was nothing to do but wait for the timer to go off and start the process. My heart was pounding so hard that I could feel its vibrations all the way from my ears to my toes.

The alarm rang and I could hear the pieces of our invention in motion, working together just like we planned. This was it—OUR MOMENT. . . .

ONLY NOTHING CAME OUT.

NOTHING BUT ...
ONE LONE KIBBLE.

We didn't know what to do. No one else did either. I didn't know it was possible for a full auditorium of people to be this quiet.

They were all just THERE.
Watching. Waiting.

FOR SOMETHING.

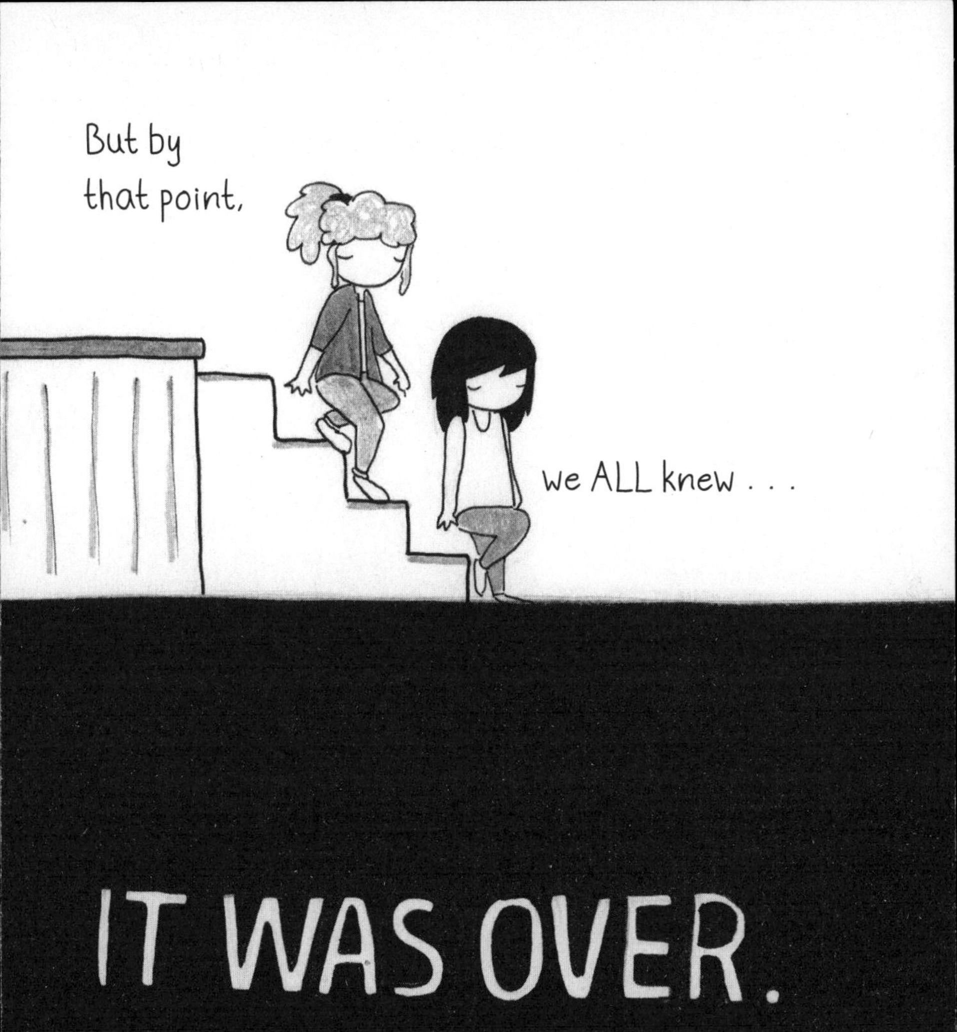

But by that point,
we ALL knew . . .
IT WAS OVER.

A hesitant pity clap broke
through the awkward silence.

It built into an uncomfortable
chorus of sympathy claps.

THAT was how tragic this was.
People didn't bother making fun of us—
they were too busy feeling SORRY for us.

As if our humiliation onstage wasn't bad enough, Mr. Walters forced us to sit and watch all the other presentations. He said it was important, as scientists, to be "good sports," but it didn't feel good at all.

I should have known—the Universe and all its laws were always against us. So what was the point of working hard if things were never going to work out anyway?

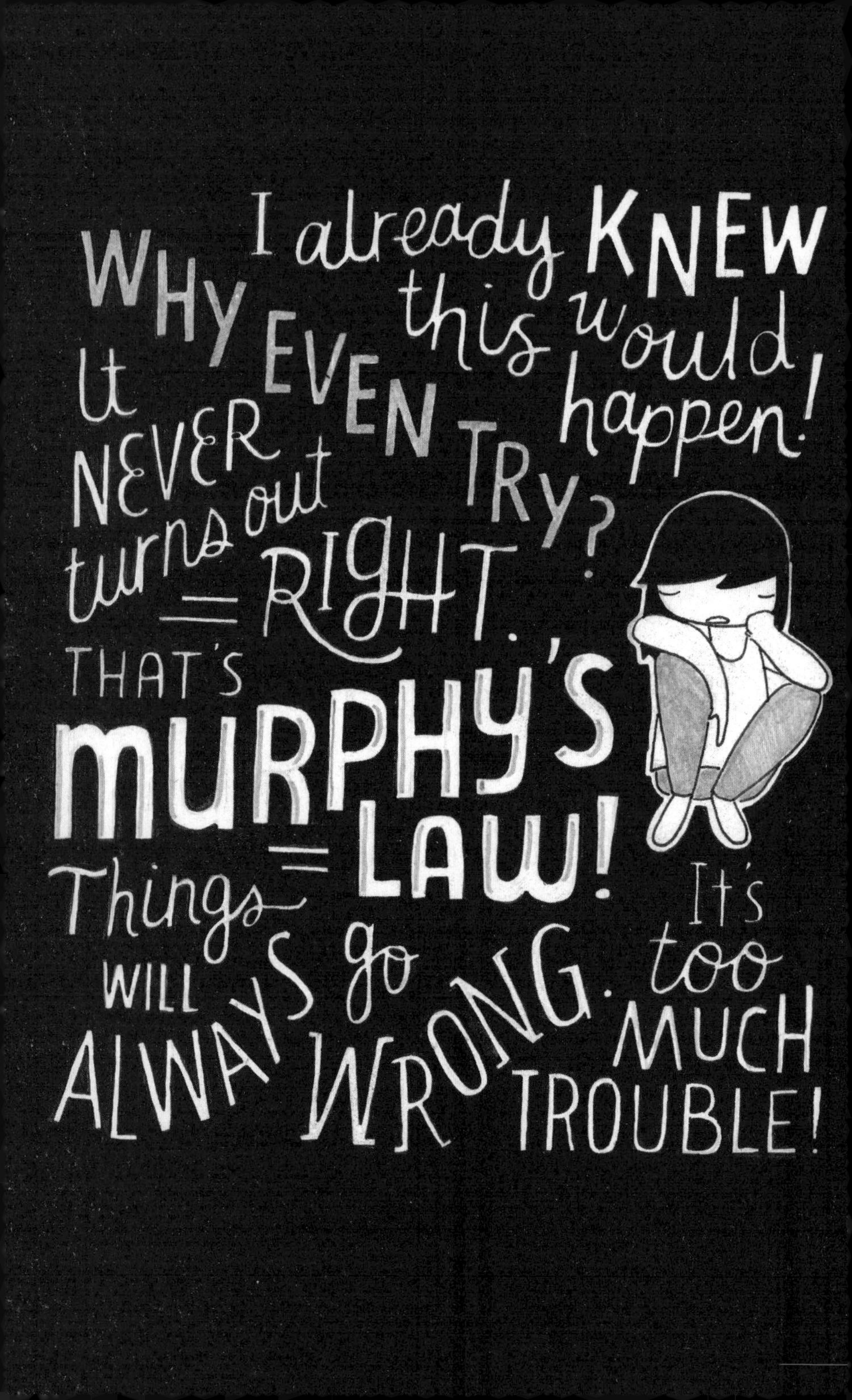
WHY EVEN TRY?
I already KNEW this would happen!
It NEVER turns out RIGHT.
THAT'S MURPHY'S LAW!
Things WILL ALWAYS go WRONG.
It's too MUCH TROUBLE!

Jess was quiet. She had been quiet the whole day. When she finally spoke, she said something I didn't understand at all.

well, WHAT'S life without A little TROUBLE?

What did that even MEAN? I had imagined all sorts of nightmare scenarios, but none of them compared to THIS reality and the truly epic failure of the FEED-IT 5000.

What other way could you possibly see it?

When I got home that night, all I wanted to do was crawl into bed, disappear under my blanket, and

NEVER COME OUT!

But before I could make it that far, Mom cornered me and asked how the presentation went.

It didn't work...

She didn't push me on it after that.

I think she could tell that I wasn't in a very good mood because she didn't nag me about finishing dinner or doing chores at all.

Peter gave me control of the remote for the night and Clara let me have the last scoop of ice cream.

Even Felix decided to give me a break.

But no matter what they did to try to take my mind off things, I couldn't help thinking about everything that had happened that day.

I kept replaying each step of the process in my head, trying to pinpoint where exactly it went wrong and what I could have done to fix it.

NOTHING.

What was the point? It wasn't just that our invention had failed. It was the fact that all our hard work was for nothing. I couldn't shake that feeling.

Jess, however, seemed to brush the whole thing off.

I didn't know if I would ever understand her. Maybe we were just TOO DIFFERENT. But if we were, could we even really be friends?

Suddenly, in the middle of all these thoughts and totally out of nowhere, Felix jumped up from his spot next to me and threw himself onto the TV screen.

There was something surprisingly true about what Clara said. It got me thinking. . . .

Maybe I just misunderstood him. I always thought Felix was out to get me and ruin things at home, but maybe that wasn't it at all.

I started to think about Jess and how differently we saw things. That didn't have to be a bad thing. I had been so caught up in trying to understand her that I hadn't really considered . . .

maybe things didn't need to be all figured out in order to WORK.

MAYBE IT ALL CAME DOWN TO →

Because, despite all our differences,
we still really got along.

PERSPECTIVE.

And THAT was
something I could
work with.

CHAPTER TEN

I was dreading school the next day, so I tried to convince Mom to let me skip it. She refused. Instead, she packed a few homemade cookies in my bag (probably as a distraction) and made sure to drop me off herself.

She told me that it was just a class project and not the end of the world, but I couldn't fully believe her.

170

After all, everyone had been there to witness our invention crash and burn. I wanted to pretend like the whole thing had never happened.

I didn't want to hear about it, talk about it, or think about it for at least a day.

So I guess, in that sense, I got EXACTLY what I wanted—except what happened next wasn't at ALL what I had in mind.

When I got to the lockers that morning, Jess was already there! I knew immediately that something was up because I usually never ran into her at our locker in the morning.

I didn't know what to say.

It SHOULD have been great.

This was what I had been wanting all along—
a space that was all my own. No more
rearranging books like Tetris pieces, no more
shoving lunches into tight corners, no more
sharing! But when she said it, it didn't feel
great.

It felt like, once again,

THINGS
WERE
CHANGING.

And I wasn't ready.

But, like a lot of changes, it happened so
suddenly that I barely had time to wrap my
head around the idea at all.

The bell rang. . . .

And we were both off to class.

That was one thing about middle school.

We were so busy trying to get through classes and figure out what was going on that sometimes it felt like there wasn't enough room in our brains to think about anything else!

As soon as I got to math class, Ms. Skelter surprised us with a pop quiz!

Then there was that particularly painful volleyball match during PE. . . .

Not to mention the horrifying video about germs that Ms. Mackey showed us in health class.

In English, Mrs. Fielding made us read scenes from this Shakespeare play called *All's Well That Ends Well*, which, in my opinion, was a weird name for a play.

(ACT II SCENE I.)

oft expectation fails, and most oft there where most it promises; and oft it hits where hope is coldest and despair most fits

huh?

It didn't even fully hit me that Jess had moved lockers until I stopped by to grab my history book on the way to class, only to realize . . . IT WASN'T THERE!

Then, it dawned on me. My book wasn't there, but I knew where it was.

It was at home—probably with all the other books I never brought to school once Jess and I started sharing a locker. I realized then that the book we had been sharing had been HERS.

She had Mr. Monroe's class in the morning and would always drop it off in the locker just in time for me to pick it up in the afternoon.

Now that history book was probably in her NEW locker with the rest of her stuff. With separate lockers, sharing books didn't really work out the way it used to.

Things had changed, and I wasn't ready.

When I showed up without my textbook, Mr. Monroe lectured me about being prepared and made me use the

CLASS COPY.

EW.

Most of the pages were ripped or covered in weird drawings or stuck together with who knows what.

As I flipped through the crusty pages of the shared class textbook, it really hit me that things would be different now.

I thought about that all through history class, and then again all through lunch when I didn't see Jess at all because the office lady, Ms. Hayes, asked her to help with some kind of boring filing project.

The next time I saw Jess that day was in science class, but since our partner projects were over, Mr. Walters decided to rearrange the class into new groups.

I started to really think about everything that was changing around me and what change meant.

I wondered what Jess thought about it all. Honestly, she was so good at dealing with change that she probably wasn't that worried.

We were VERY different.

For a while though, we figured out a way to work together and become . . . friends. But could we still be friends if all the things we shared were suddenly gone?

I honestly wasn't sure.

CHAPTER ELEVEN

At some point, I thought Mr. Walters would stop talking about the Invention Convention and move on to his next "exciting" science initiative, but he kept bringing it up ALL WEEK.

I'm so PROUD of you— all of you! You made POINDEXTER'S first ever INVENTION CONVENTION a success!

Unlike Mr. Walters, I was feeling pretty down about the whole thing.

On top of the fact that my new science group was totally unbearable, we were getting our final grades back on the invention project and I knew exactly what ours would say.

The FEED-IT 5000 had failed,
and by association,
so had we.

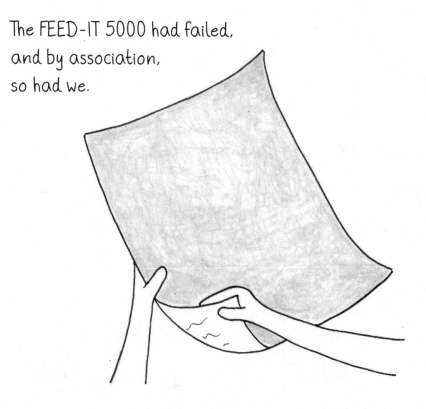

Still, I didn't want to look.

It didn't make any sense.
It had to be a mistake.

I checked to make sure he
hadn't gotten the papers
mixed up. NOPE. I added
up all the points to see if
he got the scoring wrong.
NOT THAT EITHER.

When I looked across the room at Jess . . .
she was looking right back at me,
and her face said it all—

HOW this was POSSIBLE?

As much as I liked the idea of getting an A on our project, it felt like Mr. Walters had missed something.

Jess must have had the same thought because when the bell rang, we BOTH stayed behind to talk to him about it.

When we told him why we were there, he smiled like he knew something we didn't.

IT WASN'T A MISTAKE!
(WE DIDN'T BELIEVE HIM.)

I couldn't really wrap my head around it, even after he promised us that that grade was real and that this wasn't some kind of prank.

The way I looked at it, the FEED-IT 5000 was a total DUD. So what did he see in it that we didn't?

"Your invention didn't work that day, but it's not just about that. Your presentation, your reports, your research—you did the work.
And it was good.
That counts too.

"You see, science is all about trial and error. You don't KNOW if things will work out. That's part of the process.

That's SCIENCE.
That's LIFE!

"The NOT knowing is what makes it fun."

We left Mr. Walters's classroom in a daze. It took a while for reality to sink in. Usually that meant something bad, but in this case, reality was kind of GREAT.

We had to celebrate, and there was only one proper way to celebrate something THIS good.

But not only had Jess never been . . .
she had never even HEARD of it.

I couldn't believe it!

Everyone knew that Antonia's was the best bakery in town—arguably the whole world. What kind of friend would I be if I let Jess go another day without understanding why?

I knew exactly what to do.

I mean, what else are friends for?

Once Maxine and Logan got to Antonia's, the celebration REALLY began.

Turns out, the Invention Convention had given us plenty of things to celebrate!

Maxine got the lead part in the school play! Normally, only eighth graders auditioned for those parts, but when the drama teacher saw her present her invention onstage, he offered her the chance.

This kid has STAR POWER! Get her on my stage — PRONTO!

Logan and Mira's invention was the best one in school. It was so good that Mr. Walters cried. He also submitted it to some national competition, which meant Logan was just one step closer to becoming a world-famous kid genius.

SO PROUD!!!

#1

Our invention presentation may not have gone the way we expected, but things worked out for Jess and me.

When it came down to it, we actually made a very good team, and that seemed like something worth celebrating.

Somehow celebrating turned to talking about lockers. When we asked Jess about her new one, she said—

It's great —

* EXCEPT...

It's NOT that great.

Her new locker was so far away that she had to sprint in order to make it to class on time!

It made me think about all the problems that I'd been having ever since we got our own lockers.

Even though it was what I had wanted from the very beginning, was it really better? Was it possible that things were actually better for both of us when we were sharing?

Maybe being partners had somehow caused our brain waves to sync up or something because, at that moment, I knew Jess and I were thinking the EXACT SAME THING.

We had gotten so used to sharing ONE locker—why not share BOTH?

For once, it just made sense. The only thing we needed to figure out was what to do with the other locker. . . .

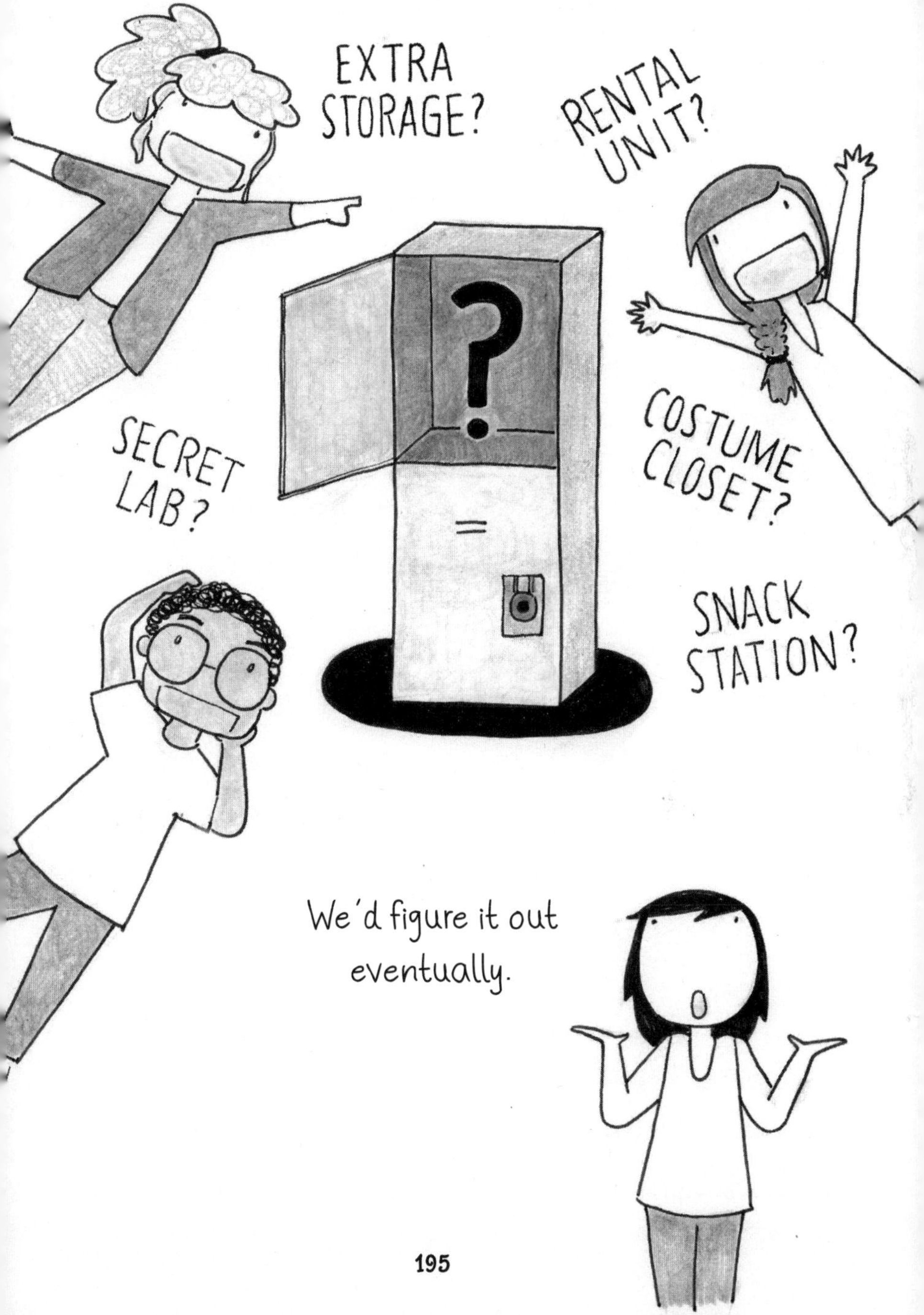
EXTRA STORAGE?
RENTAL UNIT?
SECRET LAB?
COSTUME CLOSET?
SNACK STATION?
We'd figure it out eventually.

For now, it was fun just being
at Antonia's together.

Maxine, Logan, and I were there often enough
to be considered regulars, but it was new to
Jess, and that made the whole thing feel a
little different.

Different, but *good.*

Still, being a regular at the bakery had definite
perks. Before we left Antonia's for the day,
Istvan brought over another round of pastries
to congratulate us.

Istvan wasn't just any bakery owner. He made a point of knowing everyone who came into his shop. He was probably so used to seeing the three of us that it was hard NOT to notice a fourth person hanging around all of a sudden.

"New one, eh?"

This is Jess. She's ONE OF US.

When I said it, it just felt right.

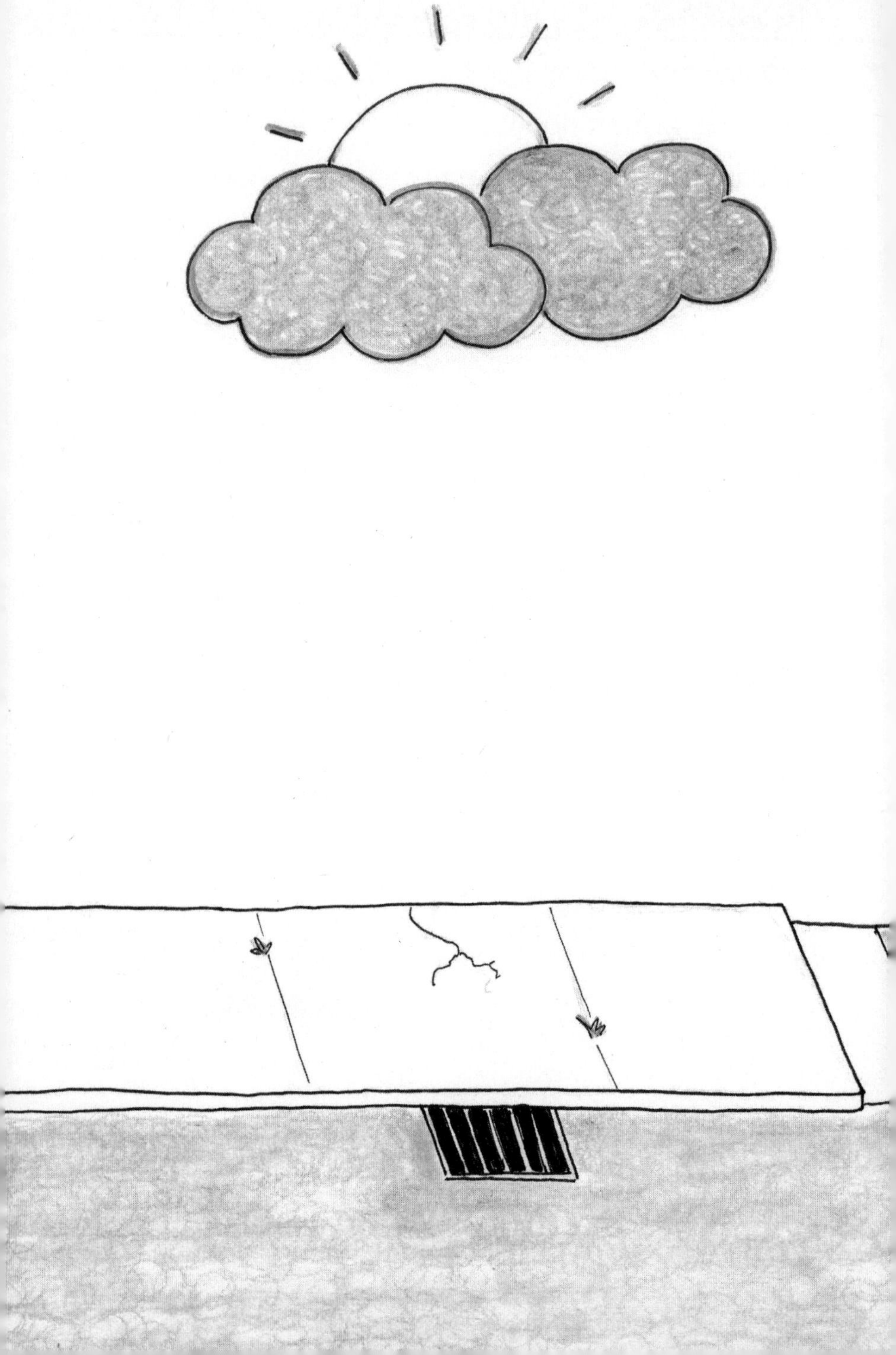

I guess, when you think about it,
some things really do work out.

CHAPTER TWELVE

A few weeks passed. By then, most of us had stopped thinking about the Invention Convention and moved on to the next crazy thing happening in middle school.

WE'VE BEEN INVADED!!!

Something crazy was ALWAYS happening in middle school.

But the FEED-IT 5000 was still on my mind!

When Mr. Walters needed space in the science lab, Jess and I played ROCK PAPER SCISSORS to figure out who was in charge of taking it.

I lost.

I should've gotten rid of it, but after all our hard work, I just couldn't bring myself to throw it away.

So the FEED-IT 5000 ended up at MY house, gathering dust in the corner of our living room.

Until one day . . .

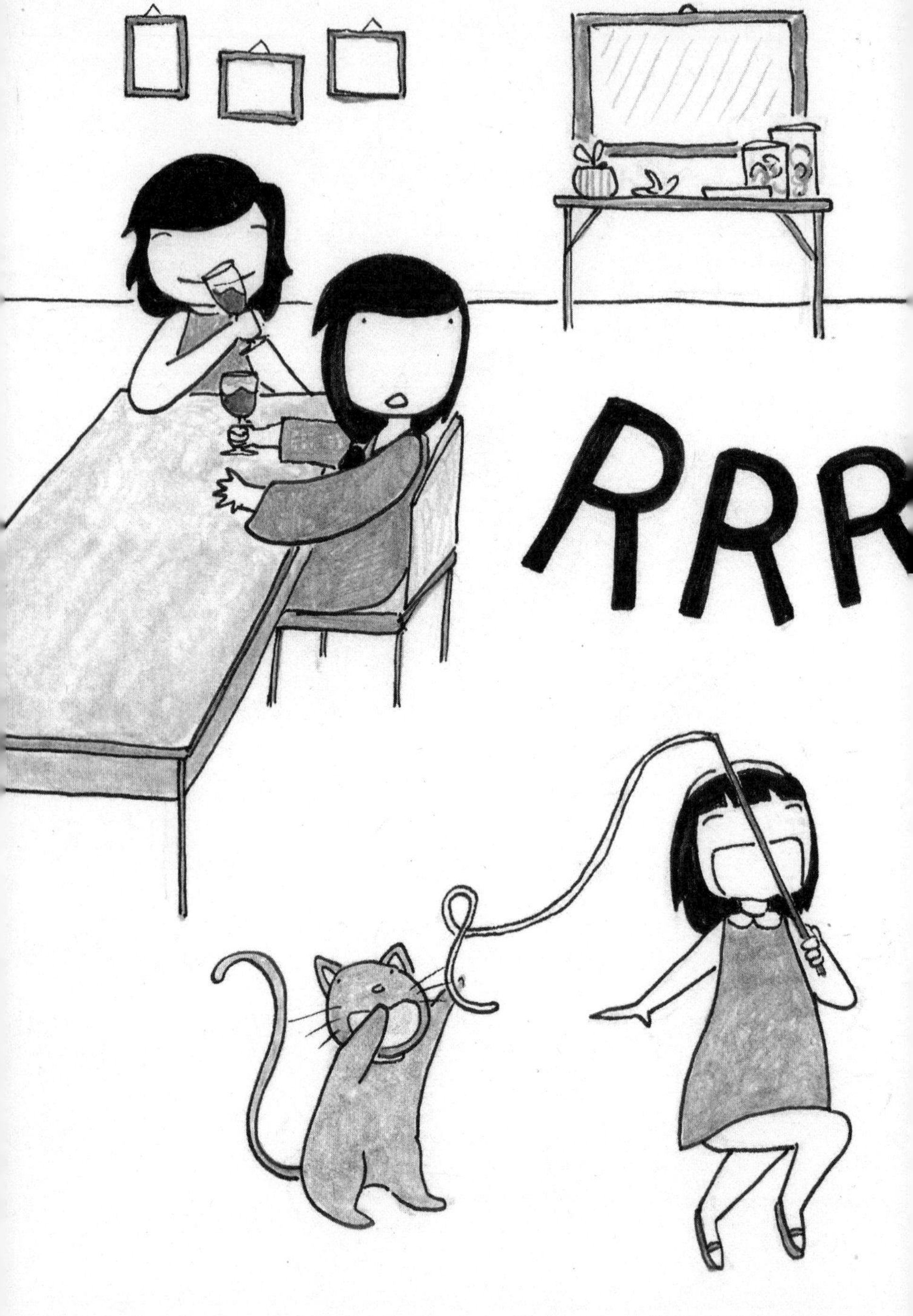
RRR

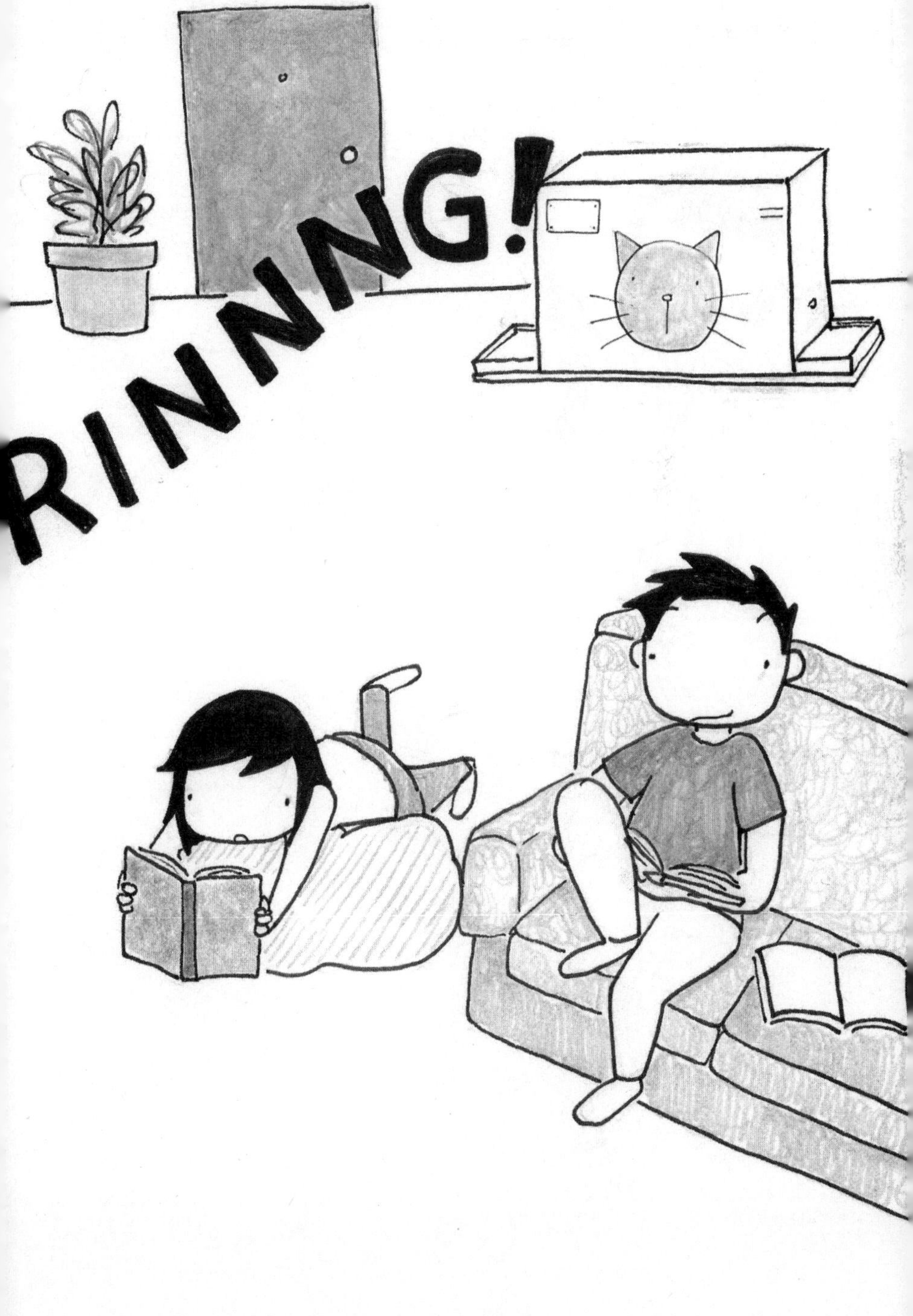
RINNNG!

It
WORKED.

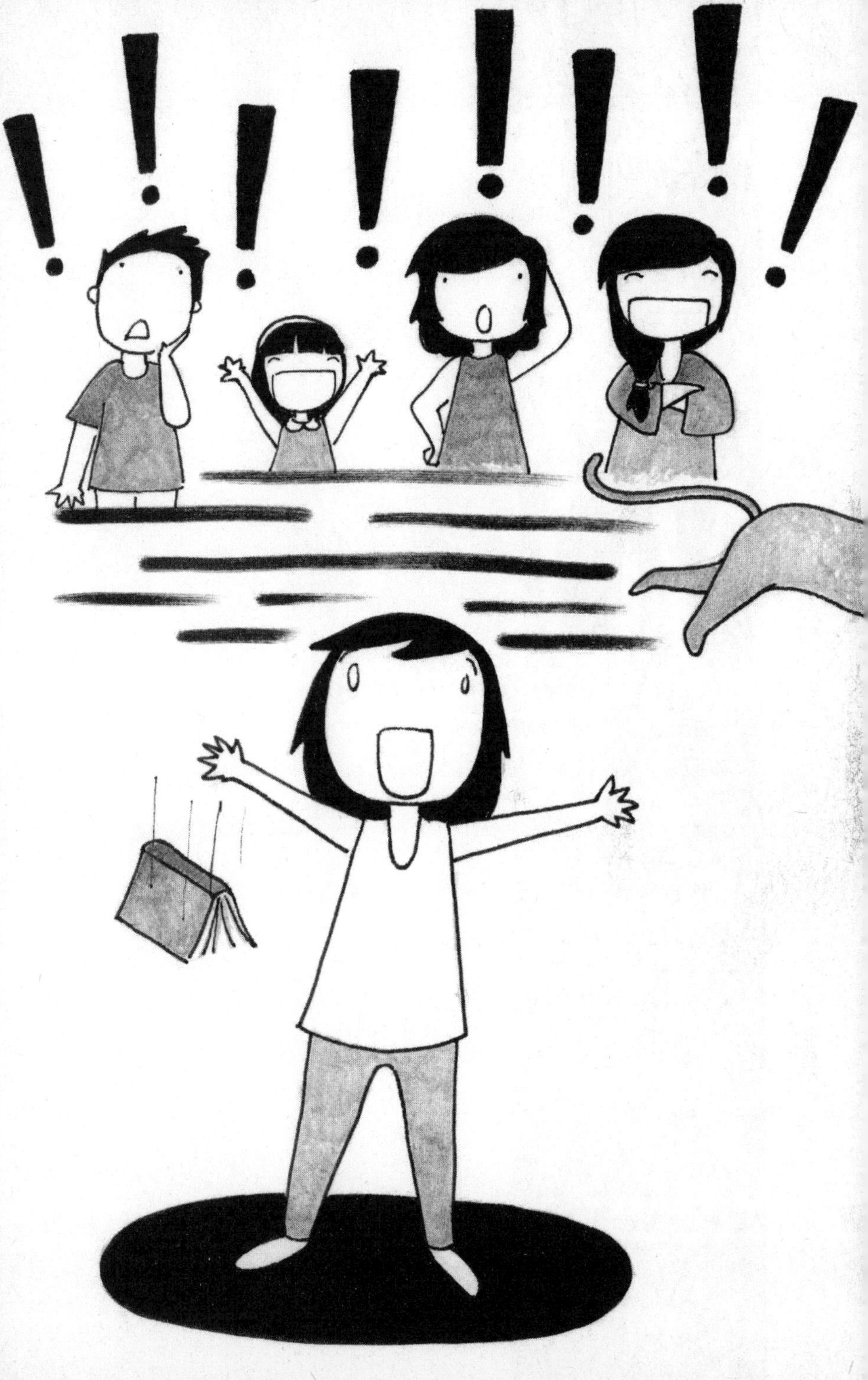

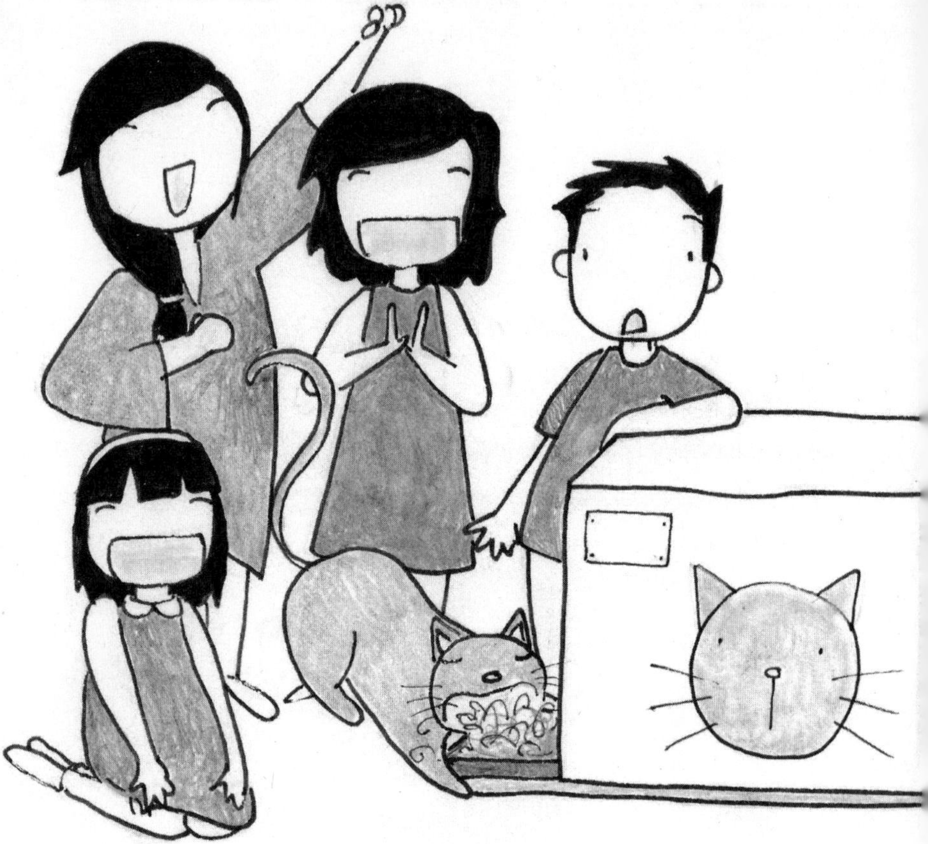

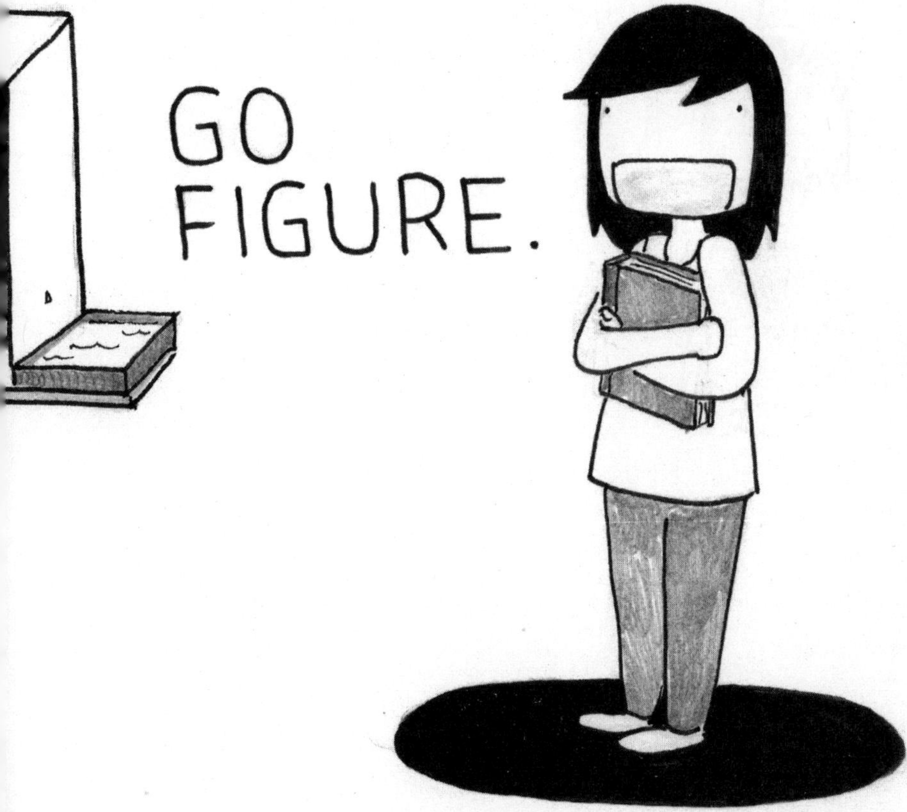
GO
FIGURE.

ACKNOWLEDGMENTS

At its core, this book is about dealing with change and finding something great in the unexpected. I wouldn't have realized that without so many of you, so here goes:

Thank you to my editor, Margaret Anastas. You bring so much joy and heart to everything Frazzled, and this book is better because of it. As always, thank you to Steve Malk for being a brilliant agent and constant source of wisdom, and Hannah, for helping me figure my way to the heart of Abbie's story.

I'm especially grateful for my publishing family at HarperCollins Children's Books:

To Amy and Andrea, for working tirelessly to transform all my ideas into an actual book and for being the designers of my dreams. To Bethany and Veronica, for reading (and rereading) my work with such astounding focus and care. To Josh and Mark, for managing the madness and somehow not killing me. To Luana, for always keeping things running.

To the unparalleled Caroline Sun, thank you for all the things and more. To my flawless publicity team, the wonderful School & Library squad, and the amazing Megan Beatie, I appreciate you beyond words.

To marketing powerhouse Ann Dye and Team Middle Grade, I always say "you're the best," and I stand behind that. Also, to Tom for creating all the best swag, Jace for making me look cooler than I am, and Elena for keeping Abbie Wu on trend. To the incredible sales team for getting Frazzled out into the world and to everyone at Harper who has been cheering for Abbie from the very start.

Thank you to all my family and friends who simultaneously embrace my craziness and keep me as sane as possible. A special thanks to Meg for providing unexpected inspiration via Szabi the cat. And, I guess, thank you to Szabi too.

Most important, thank you to my Frazzled readers. These books are always for you.

WHERE THE MISHAPS BEGAN

The *New York Times* bestseller

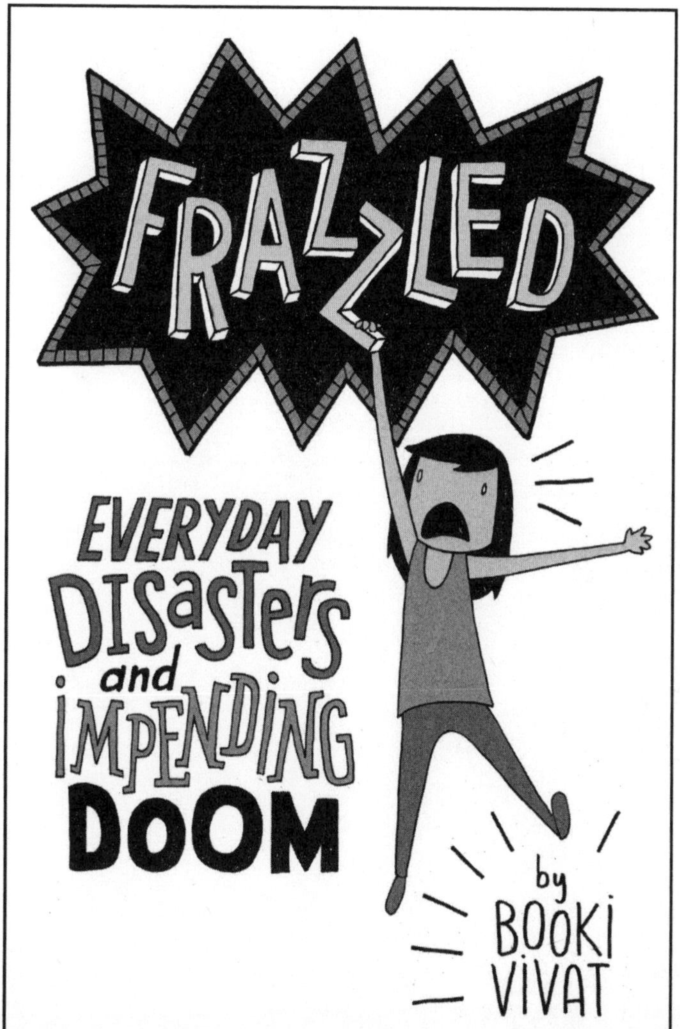
FRAZZLED
EVERYDAY DISASTERS and IMPENDING DOOM
by
BOOKI
VIVAT

Kamolpat Trangratapit

BOOKI VIVAT is the *New York Times* bestselling author of the Frazzled series. She has been doodling somewhat seriously since 2011 and not-so-seriously since childhood. She grew up in Southern California and graduated from the University of California, San Diego. She currently works in publishing and lives in Brooklyn, New York.